JUNI DAGGER

Sixteen-year-old **Arjun Chandra Kathpalia** is an accomplished piano player and a photographer from Delhi. His photographs have been featured in online photography magazines. He is also a gamer, a computer buff, a graphics designer and a gourmand. This is his first novel. You can connect with him at:

Facebook: Arjun Kathpalia

Instagram: @arjun.kathpalia

Twitter: @arjunckatz

JUNI DAGGER
MURDERS IN MERAUPATNAM

ARJUN CHANDRA KATHPALIA

RUPA

Published by
Rupa Publications India Pvt. Ltd 2017
7/16, Ansari Road, Daryaganj
New Delhi 110002

Sales centres:
Allahabad Bengaluru Chennai
Hyderabad Jaipur Kathmandu
Kolkata Mumbai

ISBN: 978-81-291-4869-8

First impression 2017

10 9 8 7 6 5 4 3 2 1

The moral right of the author has been asserted.

Printed at Nutech Print Services, New Delhi

In the loving memory of my late grandfather,
who taught me to value the written word and encouraged me
to have confidence in my dreams;
my late grandmother for her love and affection that lives on…

Chapter One

'**O**y mate! Stop the carriage right here,' said old Mr Crow. He was French but didn't sound it.

'What's the matter sir?' asked Juni Dagger. He whipped his horses once again, not for any purpose but just because it gave him pleasure.

'I see you are new to this town,' said Mr Crow.

'Indeed,' Juni replied. 'And you? What's your name again? Oh! You are the eccentric Mr Crow, yes? The "widely-acclaimed" cards player?' he enquired with a smirk.

'*I didn't know newcomers also knew my name,*' thought Mr Crow. 'You think you're better than me mister...?' asked Mr Crow.

'Juni...Juni Dagger.'

'Yeah, all that is fine, but what is your position in this town of Meraupatnam?'

'I am an investigator. And yes, I would indeed rate myself

better than you,' Juni replied.

'Yeah, an investigator looking for lost milk. Put your money where your mouth is,' Mr Crow said to some other people who had come to see what the buzz was all about. He chuckled along with them.

'No, I investigate murder and other such crimes. What's the rupee equivalent of $500?' asked Juni calmly.

'You've got some serious balls…coming into my town and challenging me like that. The initial amount is ₹10,000.'

Juni had alighted from his carriage. There were quite a few people around. One of them whisked a couple of foldable chairs and a small bamboo table from a nearby eatery. Juni and Mr Crow settled for a match. As they started playing Flash, Juni kept looking at Mr Crow, like he was observing every single detail: how he drank his water, how he asked for coffee, how he drummed his fingers on the table. After some rounds, Juni put all his money on the table. Mr Crow whistled. There was a moment of tense silence and then suddenly Juni picked up all the money and seemed about to leave.

'What the hell do you think you're doing?' Mr Crow asked.

Juni threw down his cards, a perfect sequence, 3, 4 and 5 of Spades. Before Mr Crow lowered his cards Juni said, 'A pair of Jacks for sure and a very low number I presume?'

Mr Crow showed his hand and there were 2 Jacks, and the 2 of Diamonds.

'I don't like you,' said Mr Crow in a low voice. 'Cheater!'

'Not a cheater, but an avid observer of humanity and cards,' responded Juni with a laugh. He added, 'By the way, playing cards is not a good habit, and doing it for money is even worse. Look what happened to you now. An ace player... and you lost.' He walked away.

Juni was in no hurry to plunge headlong into the case that had brought him here. Having paid off the carriage driver, he walked around in a desultory way. He liked to take things easy. He saw a cobbled street and cafés bordering each side, a few lone walkers and some couples ambling as if they had all the time in the world. The small town smelt of freshly baked bread and Indian cuisine and spices. What an eclectic mix this little town was. And then there was the occasional sound of carriages or motors moving by. Juni thought about how appearances could lie. This town had been witness to serial sniper killings. The police had not been able to even start digging into the case. And so Juni had been pressed into service.

Meraupatnam was very different from the rest of the Indian subcontinent, or the parts of it that he had seen. It seemed to be a quiet French country town that had been transported to the coast of the Arabian Sea. Being a port town, one would expect a lot of hustle and bustle. But of late, the neighbouring port town about 20 kilometres away had become the new trade centre, leaving Meraupatnam as a sleepy little beautiful coastal town. Here, things were not hectic. Everything had its own leisurely pace, so much so that when something, anything, out of ordinary happened, the town perked up its ears like a dog sleeping on a hot sunny afternoon would on hearing a sound. It would make him twitch its ears and raise its head before settling down to sleep again. This was a quiet haven with its quaint streets arranged in a grid pattern and various maisons and hotels. It seemed that huge events of history, such as the World War II and the Indian struggle for Independence, had not touched it. Some buildings showed their French heritage, while others were more neutral. Maisons and rest houses punctuated every street. It was neat beyond Indian comprehension. It was far, far away from the madding crowd. It was, perhaps, the only town in the subcontinent to have been a French colony. Since it was a port town, it also had a unique mix of ethnicities: Europeans, French Indians and Indians.

And just by looking at the locals, it was very difficult to make out if its members were French, Indian or English. The people were dressed in an interesting mix of costumes: men mostly wore trousers and shirts, and while many women would be dressed in Western attire, there were some who wore Indian salwar kameezes or saris. Most of them knew how to speak English and French apart from the local dialect. Juni wondered, '*Is this how the world may be in the future, where one's roots are submerged in a new cosmopolitan identity?*'

This was also reflected in the diverse eating places here. But lately, the spate of seemingly arbitrary killings had been like a bad recurring nightmare, disturbing this little town.

In the distance, Juni heard Mr Crow mimicking him. 'I am an investigator. No murderer shall get away from me!' Then Mr Crow burst into a guffaw.

Suddenly, Juni started running towards Mr Crow. There was the sound of a gunshot, which caused the birds to fly away. A carefully-aimed sniper gun had been fired at the man in front of Juni. He lunged forward and pushed Mr Crow to the side, and they came tumbling down.

'What was all that about?' screamed Mr Crow. Juni pointed at where the bullet had landed. Mr Crow stared in stunned silence. Then Juni got up and brushed his trousers. Then he walked away coolly. '*That shut him up,*' thought Juni.

Juni Dagger was a towering six feet two inches with a broad frame and an imposing presence. He was not very easy to miss. This was something that was often detrimental to his investigations. He had a fair complexion and wavy brown hair with streaks of gold and a jovial face that could sometimes look very threatening. His eyes were hazel, glittering green specks amid the brown. Juni looked dapper in his suit. The coat and trousers were a light grey and the waistcoat, a darker hue. The neatly ironed blue shirt peeped out with starchy arrogance.

Juni decided to head to the mayor to report to him and get his appraisal. Mayor Jacques Lebon was a middle-aged man. Tall and slender, he carried himself with an aristocratic bearing. He was always very formally dressed. Everything about him was fastidiously neat. He lived alone. Rumour had it that his daughter was in France and that he was divorced, but this was simply a conjecture. No one dared to ask him and he himself never talked about family. But he was an able administrator. The people respected him and were almost in awe of him. Juni entered his house, admiring its architecture and neatness.

'Mr Dagger, I have been waiting for you! Though I wish we had met in happier circumstances…'

Juni greeted him and after some small talk, he told the mayor of the incident with Mr Crow and the sniper. Since he was still smarting from Mr Crow's insulting behaviour, he told Mayor Lebon about his disgraceful conduct. The mayor apologized to Dagger. 'Mr Crow had some grudges against the last investigator,' he said, 'and his inefficacy.'

But Juni had lost interest in Mr Crow by now. He asked, 'Uh, where will I be staying?'

'Why, in Dormeth Lane, of course!' replied the mayor.

'Sir, but from what I have heard, that is where all the VIPs stay!'

'Exactly, I saw your records. You have skills as a bodyguard too, and staying near the important people of this town might prove helpful.'

'I will need an assistant,' said Juni.

'But don't all investigators come with assistants? Look at Sherlock Holmes and Watson or Hercule Poirot and Hastings.'

'That's not my style, I am more of a lone wolf and take and drop assistants with cases. No attachment of any sort. A rolling stone gathers no moss, as they say. Now, if you could provide me an assistant...'

'Sure, I will find the best man to help you,' said Mayor Lebon.

'I will take your leave,' said Juni. The mayor interrupted him. 'Might I ask how you saved Mr Crow?'

Juni replied, 'Simple. I saw a sniper from the corner of my eye, estimated his timing and lunged forward so that not only would Mr Crow be saved, but the sniper's efforts would go to waste and he wouldn't have time to reload the gun.'

The mayor was flabbergasted. He applauded Juni for his presence of mind. Then they parted for the day.

It had been a long day and Juni was tired with the travel, the game of cards and the sniper. He left for his apartment.

It was at a walkable distance from the mayor's house. Here, in this town, nothing seemed to be too far. Meraupatnam was indeed little and walking was the chief means of transport.

When he reached Dormeth Lane, he saw that it was breathtakingly picturesque. A row of houses with beautiful little gardens and trellises welcomed him. There was the sweet smell of jasmine mixed with roses and a cobbled street with not a speck of dirt. Juni identified his temporary home and went inside. He had a little cottage in the corner of the street. The previous residents had taken good care of the house. The house had a living room and two bedrooms, and wooden stairs leading to another set of rooms. It was nicely furnished with red-checked upholstery on the furniture and a little fireplace.

Juni sat on the sofa and enjoyed a Cuban cigar and a glass of champagne, courtesy the housekeeper who had prepared the home for him. As there was nothing to do that night, he decided to turn in early.

Chapter Two

The next morning was a chilly one. Dagger had just woken when he heard a knock on the door. '*Bonjour, Monsieur Dagger. Je suis Hugo Monroe.*'

'Whoa, don't sue me, stranger! I didn't do anything!' said Juni, pretending to be terrified.

'Oh, sorry, I didn't say "sue". I said "je suis"—it's French! Anyway, I see you do not speak Français, so to say it in English, I am Hugo Monroe.'

Dagger looked very confused. 'Your assistant,' said Monroe. He had slick black hair that was neatly arranged on his head and a pencil moustache. Both his hair and his moustache seemed to be neatly glued to his head and face. He had a sallow complexion that could have marked him out as belonging to any place in the world. He looked like he could literally disappear into thin air, so nondescript were his features. There was absolutely nothing remarkable about his appearance.

'Oh, okay so Marie…'

'Um, it's Monroe, sir…'

'Yeah…that's what I said, Monique, go get me some juice, something to eat, and the papers, go on now, scoot!' ordered Dagger. Monroe was taken aback by this strange demand from one of the world's best detectives, strange because that was not the work of a highly-trained assistant. As first impressions went, Mr Dagger seemed to be an extremely eccentric and whimsical person. How would Monroe be able to work with him? 'Heaven, help me in this assignment! Jesus, save this mortal from the tortures of a moody, mercurial and temperamental boss,' he said grimly, as he set out to do the required chores.

As soon as Monroe returned, Juni wolfed down the food. Monroe had bought some croissants and fresh orange juice. Juni and Monroe left soon after. He wanted to go to the crime scene where an attempt was made to shoot Mr Crow. He had to investigate it carefully. When he reached the intersection where the bullet had been shot, he started looking around. There seemed to be no evidence whatsoever. He was looking for the bullet but couldn't find it anywhere. On the street was a manhole. He tried to dislodge it. But then he saw the glinting metal of the bullet which had lodged itself in the corner of the manhole cover. He put it in his evidence case. Now, he looked around trying to remember. He reconstructed the scene in his photographic memory. The bullet would have been shot diagonally across from an elevated platform, where he had seen the sniper. He turned his face in that direction and zeroed in on the terrace of a building about 20 metres away from the spot.

But how had the assailant known that Mr Crow would be there at that time? Or that he would be stopping to talk to Dagger? Obviously, the bullet had been a warning for Juni. It was a challenge. Mr Crow had simply been in the wrong place at the wrong time! Juni surmised that a lot of planning had been done and the sniper, or whoever he worked for, had confidential information about him getting the case and coming to town.

When he went to the terrace, he saw that there was gunpowder all over the ledge. He heard a strange noise, the kind of which he had never heard before. 'Mary,' he shouted, 'Marie!' he bellowed again and then pointed at his assistant and signalled to him to come to where he was.

'It's Monroe, sir, and not Mary or Marie,' said Hugo, panting from climbing up the stairs.

'Yes, yes. Can you lift that for me?' asked Juni as he pointed at a wooden crate. Hugo did so and exposed a bird that fluttered away, and a metal rod. The sniper must have left in a hurry once he saw that his attempt had been foiled. Juni put the rod in his briefcase very carefully with plastic gloves which he always kept with himself and told Hugo not to touch it as it might hold some valuable fingerprints. 'That explains the noise,' Dagger said and started back for Dormeth Lane.

On the way back, he asked Monroe if he had ever had

shawarma. 'Nope,' said Hugo and so they found themselves sitting in a roadside shop with merry banners proclaiming that the 'Magic of East' would be available in a bite. Within five minutes, they were eating shawarma with expertly-arranged pita-bread wraps filled with succulent chicken and an assortment of Arabian sauces. Halfway through his, Juni suddenly got up and walked out of the shop. Monroe tried to call him back, but he was too quick and did not turn around. Hugo had to pay the bill; Dagger had taken his shawarma and his case with him.

That evening, after spending the afternoon exploring the neighbourhood, Juni went home. He opened his case and took out the metal rod. 'Aha!' exclaimed Dagger. This had to be the rod used to insert gunpowder. He took the bullet out too and studied it carefully. When Monroe entered, he told him that the rod and the bullet were from the same gun: a 7.2-calibre Mosin sample.

'How do you know that?' asked Hugo.

'Trust me, you don't wanna know,' replied Dagger. The Mosin had been discontinued in 1930. 'Hugo, give me a list of all the townsfolk older than fifty,' said Dagger.

'Now, he remembers my name,' muttered Monroe.

'What?' said Juni.

'I said, "Sure",' said Monroe.

For the next few days, Dagger went around to all the houses of people who were fifty or older and might have owned Mosins. He had the information from the city records.

He found several guns and revolvers but all the Mosin samples had their loading sticks with them and had not been used for a long time. Dagger didn't want to intrude into the lives of the citizens of Dormeth Lane as they were VIPs. Their records were also confidential and classified, and getting them would require a lot of time and bureaucratic hurdles, but they were important to the case. In fact, the mayor had been unable to help him, so he did not ask many questions. Dagger was sure that there was going to be another attack, perhaps a series of attacks, but the question was when, how and where?

Chapter Three

More than a week had passed and Juni was still trying to figure out his plan of action, when the town was rocked by another shooting. There had been another firing and this time the victim was a Mr Evans. Dagger reached the scene of the crime and set about to investigate and find some clues. 'About time,' he muttered as he picked up the bullet. The body had been buried but Dagger wasn't at the funeral. Instead, he put his time into finding the place where the sniper had been hiding. This time there was no gunpowder, just the bullet, which was the same as the last one.

The victim, Mr Evans, had been a landed gentleman who lived alone, a recluse who had long stopped interacting with other people. He met only a select few but when something irked him or his mind had had enough, he would venture out of the house and then, there was no stopping him. It was on one of those days of wandering that Juni had seen him. He had quite liked him, as Mr Evans had even offered to pay for Dagger's food. Mr Evans had not had any known enemies since he generally kept to himself. Juni was flummoxed. What was the thread that connected these killings or were they the outcome of a sick criminal mind?

Mayor Lebon was in shock. In the days that followed, he would often come to visit Dagger to check on the progress that had been made. Every day, he would ask Juni if he had found some clues, and Juni started getting more and more irritated. He was unsure how to proceed with the case.

One day, after another visit from Mayor Lebon, Juni lost his patience and shouted at Monroe, 'What have you got for me?'

Monroe was taken aback and came running out of his room. 'I recorded the dates and time of all the shots.'

Juni was surprised. He regained his composure, smoothened his hair and then said, 'Great! That could be of huge help if the killer is planning his strikes. We could find the date of his next attack. We have to crack this code!'

'There you go,' said Hugo, handing over the piece of paper to Dagger. The dates were 2, 5, 7, 9, 11, 13, 17, 16, 19 and 23.

Dagger studied them carefully. 'Yes, I know what I need— coffee and a sofa.' He sprawled his tall frame on the sofa and began studying the paper. Then his green-flecked eyes glinted and he pulled a hand through his tousled hair, sat up bolt upright and bellowed, 'Eureka! That's it.' Monroe had fallen asleep on the couch, but woke up and said, 'What? Where? Who are you?'

'Good morning Monroe,' said Dagger, his eyes sparkling while Monroe looked around sheepishly. 'Look! The first three numbers are prime numbers, then a square number, followed by three prime numbers. Then, we have the nearest square to the last number, followed by two prime numbers… That means the next assassination will be on the 29th!'

'Wow, that is one stupid killer leaving clues as if he wants to get caught!'

'No, he is not stupid. He is not leaving clues for us, he is creating a pattern because he has a target to complete; otherwise, most snipers, like ordinary people like us, would keep postponing. Take it as a deadline he sets for himself to shoot people dead!' grinned Juni. 'After all, we are now in a world of targets—business, money, companies and expansion.'

'Or he just thinks that we are plain stupid and is playing with us!' said Monroe.

'Trust me, you don't want to believe that,' said Dagger. Monroe nodded.

But Juni was feeling uncomfortable. He called the mayor to ask him to keep the security tight around the town on that date. He also finally had some clues to speak of.

'Who is calling so late at night? asked the mayor.

'It's Dagger sir, Juni Dagger.'

'Oh! Yes, it was so late that I was a little… anyway, what's the issue?'

'We need to tighten security on the 29th of this month.'

The mayor went pale with fear. 'Are you alright, sir?' asked Dagger.

'Ah! Ye-yes, I am. Just an anxiety issue…anyways, why do you say so?' asked the mayor. Juni described his findings. 'Okay,' said the mayor. 'You need to be on alert and keep me informed about what you find without any delay. Take care.'

Juni slept fitfully that night. In the morning, just as he was about to get up, he thought to himself that there must be a pattern that the killer was following in picking his victims. After a visit to the washroom, he sat down at his table and asked Monroe for the list of the people on who had been attacked. He noticed that all the people who had been targeted were residents of Dormeth Lane, and most had been government officials. 'That's a big surprise,' said Monroe sarcastically.

In the days that followed, Juni often visited the crime scenes and tried to find more clues. He waited for the red-letter day. He was going around Dormeth Lane, but to his surprise, on the 29th, there was nothing unusual, no gunshot, nothing. How could this have happened? Was the pattern that he had observed just arbitrary and not a pattern at all?

On his way home, Juni visited the police station and met Inspector Singh, a ruddy-faced man with a shrubbery of a moustache stretching across his upper lip all the way through to his mid-cheek. But the stylistic element that separated him from the rest of the lot was a huge diamond on his potato-like nose. He had twinkling eyes and a hint of belly fat under his uniform. He kept wetting his lips by sliding his tongue out, which was not a pleasant sight…thanks to his tongue piercing. Though Juni liked him at once, the inspector was not of much help.

On the way back, Juni stopped at the Shawarma Point. He decided to continue to follow the pattern. According to the pattern, the next strike would be on the 9th.

Over the next few days, Juni searched ineffectually for clues. At noon on the 9th, Juni was keeping a close watch around Dormeth Lane. He looked at the villas and cottages with their sloped roofs and pretty gardens. It was all so peaceful. '*Appearances are deceptive,*' thought Juni. But he continued assiduously patrolling Dormeth Lane. That was when he noticed an unusual movement on the top of Doriae Villa. Juni casually turned a bit and from his peripheral vision, he made out the flash of a shadow as it disappeared into a door and up the stairs.

The Doriae Villa was the only one that was unoccupied. It had external stairs leading to the terrace. Dagger went quietly up the stairs and gestured to Monroe to usher people out of the area. Juni saw the sniper ahead and waited for him to load the gun. Then he stepped forward and made a mad dash towards him. As he ran, he estimated the time it would take to disarm the sniper, evade his punch and twist his arm to get to his neck and snap the pivotal bone. The sniper turned around and saw Juni. He raised the butt of his rifle to hit him but Juni expertly evaded it and landed a blow on his shoulder.

The rifle fell from the sniper's hand and then, Juni twisted both his arms behind.

'Who are you?' asked Dagger. 'Answer me!'

The sniper replied that he worked for money.

'For money? For whom?' asked Dagger.

'You'll never know.'

Juni hesitated and then the killer continued, 'You found me, but even if you kill me, he will hire someone else.'

'You know, I have whips and wires that haven't been used for a long time. I have guns to shoot you in the knee so you will never walk again and I have every intention of doing so. Hence, you better spill all your dirty secrets,' Dagger whispered in his ears. Upon hearing this, the killer laughed and bit a pendant and collapsed. Dagger couldn't feel his pulse, and realized that he had poisoned himself. Then he put on his gloves and reached for the gun. The same Mosin gun that had been fired earlier was lying there. He took out a small foldable bag from his pocket, put the revolver in it and searched the assassin's pockets. He found nothing but some chewing gum. He opened one from its wrapper and put it in his mouth.

Juni's face was red with tension and exertion. This case was getting to him. 'Damn!' he muttered. He spat out the gum and took out his lighter and then impatiently threw that aside as well.

Juni had started to feel the urgency of time pressing on him. He was confused, tired and anxious, and didn't know where to start, what to do or where to find evidence. It was the first time that this had happened. So, to relax he went for drinks to the mayor's house even though he was not invited. But he was Juni Dagger! He would be welcomed, he was sure.

When he arrived, Mayor Lebon was surprised. 'Let him in,' he said to the guard.

'Hello, Mr Dagger. So, how is your investigation going? I heard that you are finally making some progress after being stuck and clueless for a long time,' said the mayor.

'Some hiccups along the way. I'm sure this is the only bottleneck and the rest will be smooth sailing.'

The mayor smiled and nodded. As the night went on, the burden of the unsolved murders seemed to vanish as Juni sat and had a nice dinner with Mayor Lebon.

The next morning, Dagger found himself in the guest room of the mayor's mansion. He had a splitting headache. On the way home, he found Monroe at the Shawarma Point. Dagger sat down and told him about his night. Monroe just kept nodding and eating, nodding and eating. In the middle of a sentence, Dagger stopped and said, 'Are you even listening?' Monroe nodded and took another big bite. 'What have I said till now?'

Monroe replied, 'You went for drinks, found a girl and danced the night away.'

'You sure do like shawarma, don't you?'

He nodded over a mouthful. Then, as soon as he finished eating, he ran out of the restaurant, this time leaving Dagger to pay the bill. Dagger sighed and looked at the bill. 'Eight shawarmas! Is he freaking mad? How did he run on such a heavy stomach?' Then he sighed and invited a Dutchman for drinks before the bill was handed to him, and whispered something in the ears of the waiter and ran away. The Dutchman looked frantically at the waiter when he realized what had happened.

When Dagger got home, he found Monroe sleeping on the couch. He spent hours and hours on the same set of numbers again, trying every possible way that he could think of, in order to find a code, and then finally gave up. There was nothing else he could do, or so he thought.

Chapter Four

For some time, there was a lull in the attacks. One day, when Juni was taking a walk down his lane, he saw Randy and waved to him. Randy was a thin-faced man with greying hair. His hyperactive persona could be made out at a distance. He was dressed in rumpled clothes that seemed to have never seen the face of an iron. He was not bothered about it. He was an accountant, and even though he was weird and most people laughed at him, it was his brains that kept him in the good books of his employer. He had a passion for mysteries and solving murders. He was totally into crosswords and not a single newspaper that he came across was left unmarked, its puzzles unsolved. He was following the killings. Since the mayor and Randy were childhood friends, the former trusted him completely and willingly agreed to hand him the case files. Every time something new came to the attention of the mayor, Randy would receive updates.

The fact of the matter was that Juni and Monroe were completely oblivious to this. They had no idea that the files and developments were being forwarded to another individual.

Randy absolutely loved to show off, and loved to feel a sense of superiority. Every Sunday evening, the mayor and Randy would go for drinks to the iconic Dormeth Bar which, on Sundays, always had a plethora of security guards placed outside for the two buddies. The mayor would order his drinks and Randy would have lemonade without sugar. Sunday evening was also the peak time for sandwich take-out, so Juni often came by to eat some sandwiches and then rest in his cottage.

One serene Sunday evening, about a week after he had seen Randy, Juni came home panting, and from his face one could tell that he was mortified.

'What happened?' asked Monroe.

Juni replied in a slow and dramatic tone, 'The sandwiches.'

'What about them?' asked Monroe who was now starting to feel the heat. People of Meraupatnam had started questioning him about their inability to solve the case. They were making a lot of enemies.

'They are over!' lamented Juni. There was a maddening silence as both knew what this implied. 'Do you know what this means?' asked Juni.

'I'm afraid I do, it means that…' Monroe stuttered and then continued, 'that there will be no sandwiches tonight.'

They stared at each other for a while. 'I need a drink,' they said in unison. They went to Dormeth Bar.

'Juni, this is Randy, my close friend and accountant. Randy, this is Juni, our lead detective in the recent case,' the mayor introduced them. Juni, being completely sober, shook Randy's hand and exchanged a few words of greeting. However, Juni knew that Randy didn't like him and he even noticed that he was looking at him weirdly.

Randy looked at Juni and then at the mayor and said, 'Why did you need to bring him when I was already here? You know that I can solve the mystery.' He sounded very miffed and peeved. The mayor placated him and said, 'We have been through it so many times before Randy. Well, I just wanted to see what the "better among the best" could do.' He gestured towards Juni, who felt a passing discomfort but then chose to ignore it. 'Randy,' he said, 'Why don't you solve another mystery and prove your worth?'

Randy looked at him disdainfully. 'You think I should play with cars while you take on the rockets? No sir! Not happening! You will see how I am quicker than you at solving this!' He gulped down his lemonade and Juni noticed that he kept moving his left hand near his ear and back again. He felt a twinge of pity for this man and decided to let things be.

After some time, the mayor got up to use the washroom, leaving them alone.

'So, how much do you know about the case?' asked Randy.

Juni replied, 'Not much, we haven't got any recent leads,'

which wasn't true as he had the series of dates from the crime scenes.

Randy knew that he was lying and said, 'What about the series of dates that you are trying to crack?'

Juni didn't wait and straight-up dive-tackled Randy and cuffed him, kicking him in the arse and reading him his rights. The mayor entered and saw this rather funny situation as poor Randy was trying to break his thin French-fries-shaped hands, free of the metal cuffs. Resisting the urge to laugh, the mayor demanded an explanation. Monroe replied, telling him that Randy had classified information on the case. The mayor instructed Juni to uncuff Randy and proceeded to explain how he had been giving him all the details. Juni did so, but objected to his giving information without his consent. Randy, meanwhile, was throwing a fit claiming that he could have died after such a 'takedown'. Juni wasn't listening to any of what he was saying and likewise, the mayor and Monroe turned a deaf ear, knowing that he was just whining. But then, Randy started shouting that he would solve the case before Juni and teach him a lesson. Saying this he left with the mayor, who was trying very hard to placate him.

Juni had had enough. He ate some chicken steak and headed home. The bill wasn't presented to him, obviously, since he and Monroe had been with the mayor.

Chapter Five

Days went by and Juni and Monroe had not found any significant leads. They would often talk to people and try to glean information but it was as if things were in slow motion.

One evening, Juni sat in the living room with his coffee, looking out of the window at the riot of colours that the flowers had made in the little garden. He saw a sudden movement and a fleeting shadow. Who could it be at this hour? Dagger decided to check, and went out just to have a flying star thrown at him, which pinned his clothes to the door. '*I did not see that coming,*' he thought. He saw a person walking up to him. 'It must be a ninja. I mean, who else goes around at night throwing metal stars at people?'

But it turned out to be a girl in black.

'Shouldn't you have black bandages all over your body like a mummy?' he asked.

'Well, I don't have them, so why don't you get yourself a nice hot cup of shut-the-hell-up?' said the girl.

'Funny girl,' said Dagger.

'What are you doing here at this hour of the night?' asked the girl, to which Dagger replied, 'Shouldn't I be asking you that?'

'Listen up birdbrain, I am a trained assassin hired to kill and make it look like an accident, so answer me right now!'

Dagger sighed and still there was not a hint of fear in his tone, neither did he break a sweat. The girl removed her shuriken and twisted Dagger into a hold in which she could have snapped his neck.

As the girl started to snap his neck, he turned his body and twisted the girl's arm behind her back and said, 'Listen up assassin, I am the detective of this town and I don't want any bullshitting.' He dragged the girl into his house. Monroe got up and saw Dagger dragging a female into the house. He shouted, 'Are you mad? We are detectives; we have to maintain our reputation!'

Dagger hushed him. He tied the girl to a chair and took out his revolver.

The girl said, 'So much safety for a girl,' to which Dagger replied, 'Not for a girl, for a trained assassin hired to kill. Now, what's your name?'

'Anna,' she replied.

'So, we have to do this the hard way,' said Dagger. 'Your name is Cameron.'

'How do you know?' asked the girl.

'It's written on your bag birdbrain! Are you the one going around killing people?' asked Dagger.

'We can't talk here,' said Cameron.

'Yeah right. I know what you mean, now, spill!' said Dagger.

While the interrogation was underway Monroe stared blindly at Cameron.

Cameron asked for a paper and pen, and then wrote on it, 'Your house is wired with a microphone.'

That would explain many things, but Dagger did not buy it. Instead, he asked her how she knew, to which she again wrote down that the wire went around the fan and the switch was just too thick as compared to a normal wire.

Dagger cracked open the covering of the fan to see another wire going under his desk. Cleverly taped there was a microphone. He broke the microphone and asked the same question. Cameron slipped out of the ropes without strain. Monroe jumped in his seat and Dagger told him calmly to sit down.

'Do you seriously think that I am an assassin? That I would use guns?' Her dark brown hair was tied neatly in a ponytail, and she had extremely intelligent eyes. A slim athletic and lithe frame with sinewy muscular strength told its own story of intense physical training. Cameron had a point about guns, Juni concluded but he decided to keep a watch on her. She tugged Dagger's hand and took him outside. They walked to her place with Dagger, who had a revolver, keeping a close eye on her. Cameron's house was not very far but was in a more modest neighbourhood. As she went inside Juni decided to hover around for some time. After about an hour or so, when he did not see anything untoward, he started walking back to his cottage where he had to answer some questions that came from Monroe.

At home, he decided to take it easy. He was in a languorous mood. It had been an unusual encounter with a very attractive girl. He thought of listening to some music. As he turned the tuning knob of the radio, he intercepted a very strange and never used frequency. The man at the other end was shouting about some unfinished task. He was issuing instructions to someone. Juni listened, amused till he heard the words, 'Carry on with the rest of the kills.' And then suddenly the language switched to Russian.

The speaker was shouting but Juni couldn't understand. Juni was on high alert but could not glean much. He rubbed the stubble on his chin. Somehow, the radio frequency had interfered with the telephone conversation. That meant the killer was not very far.

He told Monroe and the mayor about this and Monroe prepared a list of people who spoke Russian. The next day, even though he tuned into the same frequency, nothing unusual happened.

The days were passing fast. Dagger was not progressing as fast as the mayor would have liked. One day, as Dagger was walking in the lane lost in thought, a voice hailed him, 'So, an investigator for stolen milk is also too big a task for you eh?'

He turned around and saw Mr Crow.

Juni sighed, 'I should have guessed.'

Mr Crow came closer to him and clapped his hands and shouted, 'A gunshot, a gunshot, go on investigate!' Juni looked at him and started laughing. Mr Crow had a bald head and round glasses. He seemed to be peering out of them each time he looked. But his confidence in himself actually made him a daunting persona. Juni told him to take it easy.

Mr Crow said, 'Easy when all you are bothered about is food and escaping restaurant bills. I am in danger! A bullet was shot at me…'

'May I remind you that it was I who saved you?'

Mr Crow spluttered in anger and said, 'You are so rude and lacking in civility. How dare you remind me of unpleasant things?'

Juni looked at him in wonder. Was this what was known as humanity—a set of ungrateful, comical, grotesque characters living in unabashed arrogance and self-delusions? Suddenly, he heard a familiar voice greeting him. It was Cameron. He hurried to meet her.

'Am I glad to see you! Have you ever had shawarma?'

She replied, 'No,' and they ended up at the Shawarma Point. Dagger would try to stay with her so that he could get to know more about her and have her blurt out what she might have been trying to hide. But she seemed to genuinely not be a part of the killings. She also looked deceptively innocent in a pink floral dress. Juni took a quick look at himself in the window's glass. He didn't look too bad himself. His hair was a little messed up but he had given up on it a long time ago. His arms looked thick and strong. '*Oh! Wait; was that a bit of my tummy popping out? I would have to take care of it*,' he thought.

Juni asked Cameron, 'What were you doing that night?'

'Trying to find the murderers.'

Juni hesitated and then said, 'Why don't we try to do it together?' Cameron agreed and put down her rules.

- Never talk at home.
- Don't include Monroe.
- Pretend we are in a relationship.

Dagger was not too comfortable with the rules. But he kept his mouth shut.

By the time they had finished talking, it was early evening. Juni was feeling a bit hungry. Suddenly Cameron asked, 'Have you ever had pies?'

'Are you kidding me?' replied Juni. 'Pies? Who hasn't eaten a pie?'

'Yes…but have you ever had pie?' asked Cameron cryptically again.

'No,' lied Juni.

'So, let's eat.'

They went to a restaurant that Cameron had discovered. It was a little place—just a fifteen-minute walk from Juni's cottage. It served just the best pie that Dagger had ever tasted.

'What is your progress on the case?' asked Cameron.

'How can I trust you?' counter-questioned Dagger.

'You can't,' replied Cameron. 'But you can't trust Monroe either. You can't trust a single person, but you need help. Whoever the killer is, he or she is going to the extent of bribing, killing, installing microphones so neither are you safe nor do you have complete privacy. So spill the details.'

Dagger told her about the pattern of the dates, the details of the gun, and his encounter with the sniper. He did not speak of the notes and clues that he had received because he didn't want to risk it. Also, the killer didn't know about them, and if Cameron was on the side of the killer, then this information could be kept safe.

Cameron absorbed all the details and went off in a flurry, leaving Dagger to pay the bill. Dagger was bemused. He invited a Meraupatnam local to dine with him, and pretended that he was informing him of the course of the investigation and then ran away, again!

On his way home, someone in an oversize beige coat bumped into Dagger and dropped a piece of paper. Dagger didn't consider chasing him as he had eaten a lot and then run out of the eatery. He was feeling lazy and decided to read the note instead. It said:

Find him; it won't be hard!
Accuse him; well, you could be shot!
Catch him; impossible it is!
Only if you find evidence and witnesses, can you not be
considered a pawn!
Against this treachery by the lover of prawn...

Dagger went home. Monroe was waiting for him. He was quite annoyed at having been left behind. They sat in the little garden and tried to decipher the poem but couldn't come up with any valuable inputs.

Juni was inactive for the next few days. He took time off to find out more about the people of Meraupatnam, to cut people off the suspect list. He started with the pie restaurant owner, who was always in the restaurant. Also, he was a retired military general, so he could talk about guns and firepower.

Juni didn't talk to Cameron during this time but then suddenly met her at the pie restaurant. As they sat, Cameron asked, 'So, how is the poem coming along?' Juni was really surprised. 'How do you know?' he asked suspiciously. Cameron said airily, 'Oh, the word gets around.' Juni was looking extremely uncomfortable by now. Cameron said, 'Relax! When you were busy evading the bill with the local, I was observing all that happened from a corner to make you understand that even when you are trying to get free meals, someone is always watching you!' Juni had recovered his composure by now. He grinned sardonically, 'Good for you! Now that you know about the poem, let's talk about it. Shall we?' They discussed it again and again, but could not come to any conclusion.

Juni decided to inform the mayor of the developments. On hearing of the riddle, he banned the sale of prawns. 'But why would you do this? I don't think it's needed,' said Juni, but the mayor said that he was just being helpful and cautious. The rich and important people in the town had decreased in population by 15 per cent (actually 14.5 per cent). Some had been killed whereas many had left the town. Maybe if prawns were banned, the killer would become desperate and come out of hiding. The mayor seemed sure of this, though Juni was not sure it would make a difference.

As Juni was walking back home, one day, he saw a rosy-cheeked woman talking to Mr Crow. Was she rosy-cheeked or was she blushing? She had an infectious laugh and looked extremely cheerful. Her hair was curly and she looked like a very satisfied and happy woman. Juni thought that she was happy because she was single. He grinned and decided to take his revenge on Mr Crow.

He nonchalantly approached them. Mr Crow looked at him with thinly disguised irritation.

'So Mr Crow, this must be your daughter! Hello, Miss…?'

'Lilly,' said the girl.

'What?' exclaimed Mr Crow. 'I'm not her father!'

'Why Miss Lilly, you look so young!' continued Juni, ignoring Mr Crow.

Lilly, now blushing, said 'Why, I am! What made you think otherwise?'

'Well, considering you are with this old man, I thought...'

'What?! How dare you!' continued Mr Crow.

'Oh, no, I was just asking for directions!'

Mr Crow was now red with anger.

'I'll guide you, milady.'

'Why thank you Mr...'

'It's Dagger, Juni Dagger.'

She smiled and they moved away, leaving Mr Crow furious and red-faced. He was sputtering with rage as Juni walked away with Lilly.

Mr Buchner was standing in a corner watching the scene. Lilly was not very young but was remarkably fit and most importantly, single. She had all the single men of various ages eating out of her hand. Mr Buchner had been trying for a long time to get ahead of Mr Crow but Lilly had a flair for fending people off and keeping them waiting. Mr Buchner sighed and prayed for a time when he could get his beloved Lilly to notice him.

Chapter Six

As days passed, Juni grew more and more resigned to the idea that something more was needed to crack the case. The cryptic message was teasing him but he could not figure out its meaning. He was on tenterhooks as he was worried about another strike. This did not bode well for his record as a special agent and investigator.

Days turned into a month and an uneasy calm prevailed. Dagger was not surprised. He had a gut feeling that belied rational expectations. He kept thinking about the cryptic message but could not draw any conclusions. He could not leave the town without solving the crime mystery. And the mayor was losing patience fast.

Monroe felt there was something strange about Dagger's behaviour. Cameron had just come back after being missing from the town for a few days. She was moving in and out of the room with a nervous energy. Dagger thought that he really should not trust Cameron. She was obviously no gentle fairy. But even though his mind raised doubts, he felt that she could be trusted, that she was not someone who would harm others, extremely smart and worldly wise though she may be. But Juni thought that there was no proof as to his opinion. 'So much for hunches and gut feelings, if I am wrong then God save us!' muttered Juni to himself.

One day, while Cameron and Dagger were discussing topics not related to the case, she brought up the question of Dagger's marriage. 'You are as daft as a bush,' said Juni. Cameron replied, 'Merely asking about your marital status makes me daft?'

'Are you crazy?' exclaimed Dagger.

Cameron laughed and said, 'You realized that I am barmy, now?'

'Women and sarcasm,' Dagger said.

Their few moments of normal conversation were interrupted by Monroe when he came into the room and showed them the newspaper, with the headline: 'Killer strikes again: renowned detective termed as a skidder.'

Dagger was outraged, so he went to gather some firearms. Then he asked for a meeting of all the Dormeth Lane residents. It was an emergency meeting arranged for that evening.

As all the residents came together in the Town Hall, special security was put in place. Otherwise, they would have been an easy and a soft target for a sniper. As Juni ascended the podium to speak on the mike, there were sounds of hooting and booing. A voice that sounded like Mr Crow's taunted him about being a loser. Another asked him if he liked pies or shawarmas and then people started calling him a deceiver.

Juni spoke with authority and said, 'People of Dormeth Lane. Yes, I love pies and shawarmas but that does not mean that I am not good at my job. And to prove it, I shall catch the killer very soon. But you must follow my instructions. You must stay in your homes most of the time and enlist someone to walk as a human bait.'

There was a buzzing in the crowd, and then an uneasy silence. No one seemed keen to volunteer.

Mr Buchner, still suffering from the pangs of unrequited love, thought that this would be a great opportunity to impress Miss Lilly. He first looked at the crowd and sidled near Lilly, and then boldly stepped forward. 'I will volunteer on behalf of this town. I am ready to risk my life,' he said, looking straight at Lilly.

Lilly looked at him as if she had seen him for the first time. 'Eh yes, Mr Buch..'

'No, no! Harry for you, always Harry for you!' gushed Mr Buchner. Lilly looked impressed. Harry Buchner glowed with pride. He had finally scored over Mr Crow. This was how heroes are made. This was how legends were born to be remembered for posterity.

Dagger, on the other hand, knew that this plan was fraught with danger but he was running out of options. The killer had to be lured out of his hiding. He had also to prove to the townsfolk that he was a serious detective who meant business, and that he was no lazy sod. They decided to try the plan for about a week or so. Dagger set up a team of sharp shooters who would be deployed in the danger zone, including Cameron and Monroe. They were instructed to shoot on sight if they saw the killer. Dagger knew that the only way to solve the mystery was to catch the killer alive, but that seemed too distant a possibility.

Some days passed, but nothing seemed to be happening. Mr Buchner would walk up and down the lane, into its lonely and quiet corners. Occasionally, he would see Ms Lilly and those days he thought that the effort was worth it. On the fifth day, as Mr Buchner was walking up and down Dormeth Lane, Cameron, who was hiding in an abandoned building saw through her binoculars a flash of metal. In a split second, she reacted and shot in the direction where she had seen the flash. There was a loud thud and the body of an assassin fell out of the window of the same abandoned building. Mr Buchner collapsed and had a bout of shivers. Lilly, who was nearby buying groceries, rushed to him but he was too shocked to notice her. Mr Buchner had to be carried to his house. Lilly accompanied him all the way.

Cameron said that using human bait was too risky. The bait could have died of a fear-induced heart attack and then the onus would be on Juni. Also, no one would volunteer after seeing Mr Buchner's shock. There was no surety that the incident would help Mr Buchner's love story.

The next day's headline read: 'Killer dead—Investigator and team saved man.' Juni started trying to formulate a second plan to catch the killer alive, and then it came to his mind, 'tranquillizing guns'! Well, this idea should have come to his mind some time ago, but he had been too 'preoccupied'.

Juni tried to buy tranquillizing guns but they were banned in the town. While eating a slice of delicious chicken and mushroom pie, he asked the owner about it, since he was a retired military general.

General Nolheim very calmly replied, 'Take mine.' Dagger stared, astonished, even as the man went in and brought out a gun and gave it to him. Dagger nodded and thanked him.

Juni felt that he was now adequately armed. He and Cameron would patrol the streets, newly armed. He felt that it was much more interesting to pass time with Cameron than with Monroe. They spent days trying to look for suspicious elements, but to no avail. Juni looked around slightly disheartened. The children played hopscotch, the flowers smiled, and all seemed fine with the world.

One day, Juni was feeling frustrated sitting at home. Suddenly, he announced to Monroe that the next two shooters would first, be tranquillized. Then, mercilessly tortured and only later, killed. Monroe asked the reason for this to which Dagger replied, 'Don't act like a git.'

'No seriously, why would you do this?'

'So that the next killer we catch knows what will happen to him if he does not cooperate.'

'That's it?' asked Monroe, seeming shocked.

'Yes, what did you think?'

'I thought that it would have a deeper meaning,' said Monroe.

'That's the problem. Life is simple and random—Take it at face value—Tit for tat! The killers showed no mercy and they were only on a contract. The real Satan is still out there and we talk of mercy! No, no let's keep it all simple. That's the best thing to do.'

'And what about a deeper meaning? You look so serious and work so hard, as if you are breaking some complex codes. I get petrified looking at you.'

'But serious and simple are not opposites!' said Juni.

Just then Cameron entered the room, breaking off their seemingly pointless conversation.

'What have you got for me?' asked Dagger.

'Not much, just wondering whether your decision of telling the mayor about me working with you is a good one.'

'Why?'

'The mayor loves drinking alcohol and this crucial information might slip out of his mouth at an inopportune moment.'

'I agree, but if you want to be recognized and paid, then we have to let him in the loop, officially!' said Dagger.

The three of them hadn't eaten shawarma for a long time now, so they decided to go to the Shawarma Point. As Monroe was pulling out his wallet and asking Cameron to split the bill, Dagger said that he would pay. 'WHAAaaaaaa?' exclaimed Monroe in confusion. Cameron seemed shocked too and they remained quiet till the bill was paid and the waiter was thanking Dagger for not asking another stranger to look after it.

'It's been days and we haven't discussed anything about the case,' said Cameron. They began walking home. Suddenly, Dagger threw Monroe out of his way and pulled Cameron close. They were quite puzzled but then he crouched on the ground and a bullet went whizzing past.

'I did not know who the bullet would hit but I knew that this was going to happen,' he explained.

'How?' both asked him at the same time.

Dagger smiled and said, 'I don't drink that much.'

Cameron and Monroe were blushing. Cameron said, 'But I thought that you loved alcohol!'

'Oh, on normal days it's the best thing ever, but on days like these where the threat can come from anyone or anywhere, I prefer to remain sober.'

Juni collected the bullet and took it home. The following day, he gave Monroe the bullet to prepare a ballistics report as he was the only one with adequate knowledge of machine guns and pistols. Monroe told Dagger that this kind of bullet was not allowed in the 'noble town' of Meraupatnam.

In this town, there is not much security so a gun could be stolen or smuggled very easily,' thought Dagger.

Having reached a stage where something decisive had to

be done, Dagger decided to disguise himself. He had another plan. He took out his paraphernalia: a blonde wig and some interesting moustaches. Now, he surveyed himself—yes, the tattered jeans and sleeveless vest were a far cry from his usual formal self. He went to the gun shop. He asked the manager if he had a 40-calibre full-iron cobra gun, the kind whose bullet he had found. The gun was not available in the town. But the shop manager gave him a card with another address.

Dagger went to that address. It was a little nondescript shop located in the bi-lane of a bustling street. The door was shut and there were curtains over the windows. Juni knocked and then turned the handle. It was open. As he was going to talk to the man behind the counter, a door opened in the dark corner of the shop and out came Randy. Juni gave an exasperated grunt. Randy grinned at him but pretended not to recognize him. Before Juni could say anything, he had disappeared. Juni decided that he had to tackle the man before he tackled Randy.

The man behind the counter was looking at him but Juni was a great impersonator. He looked like a street hoodlum. Juni bought a 40-calibre python, because the man behind the counter said that he did not have a cobra. It had been sold. 'To whom?' asked Juni. 'None of your business!' replied the man brusquely.

Juni walked to the door and locked it from inside. The man behind the counter said, 'What do you want? I have given you the gun you asked for!'

'I want my money,' said Dagger.

'Get out!' said the man. Dagger moved at lightning speed, and took one of his arms and twisted it behind him, pinning him to the wall. Then he handcuffed him. He seated him in a chair and said in a calm manner, 'Well, you did not give me my money back, so now you gotta spill the beans. Where did you get the cobra from and who did you sell it to?'

He took out his pincers and moved purposefully towards the man. The man flinched and screamed, 'No, no, no, no pain! I will tell you.'

The man said that the client had talked spoken in a whisper and he could not make out his face, but he knew that he was tall. Since he had had an overcoat on, he couldn't make out his build. He could have been well built, but the man was not sure.

'Where are the sales records? Did he sign?' Juni asked.

The man took out some bills and showed them to the detective. Juni saw a rough illegible scribble. The only letters he could make out were m and y or v.

Dagger left the shop and rushed home. He prepared another list of people who spoke Russian and whose names had the letters M, Y and V.

Dagger was feeling overwhelmed and overworked so he sat back and discussed the situation with Cameron and with her approval had let Monroe in with the confidential matters.

Later that evening, Dagger, Cameron and Monroe went to the Shawarma Point. He told both his helpers to repeat after him, 'Oh, Almighty! Give us the power to control our food habits. Tonight shall be the last time we overeat. From now on, we solemnly swear that we will eat healthy.'

Monroe did not like this pledge but he knew that he had to lose a couple of pounds. They ate like crazy and then they promised not to eat that much again, ever.

Chapter Seven

Some days later, all the citizens of Dormeth Lane were summoned to the Town Hall for an auction. The mayor had put out a notice to this effect. Now, looking rather slim, the mayor stood at the microphone and announced the commencement of the auction: 'Surprise auction of old artefacts!'

Dagger was sure that the killer would strike that day, so he ensured maximum security and was personally on guard. From the corner of his eye, he could see Randy. He checked every single one of the citizens personally. Monroe was to ensure security inside the hall. Cameron was their emergency sniper located at the top of the building opposite the only entrance left open; all the other entrances were sealed. With this much security, Dagger was almost sure that nothing could go wrong, but then they could not take chances. He was outraged by the mayor's carelessness in organizing an event in which all the citizens who were in danger were gathered under one roof.

Dagger was perspiring and tensed. His shirt was wet and sticking to him uncomfortably. His face looked stern. He made occasional rounds of the hall while the auction was underway. On his fifth or sixth round, he noticed a man with a huge square stomach. He went closer to get a better look but was summoned by the mayor.

The mayor wanted an update. He also wanted special privileges for his bodyguards, who were finally allowed in without being frisked. Dagger almost exploded at such critical time being wasted and started fantasizing about all the torture through which he would subject the mayor to a slow death. While doing so he quickly ran out to find the square-bellied man. He still seemed to be walking around aimlessly. Dagger decided to throw caution to the winds, and went straight to him and pinned him to the ground. Then, he started to strip-search him. People were shocked, and women pretended not to look while at the same time surreptitiously glancing at the man who was being searched. A collective gasp stopped Juni just in time.

Unfortunately, his fears were proved true; the square tummy was not due to the lasagne that he might have eaten, but a live bomb that would detonate in five minutes! Juni released him and took a step back.

The man had started screaming in fear, as Juni announced that the bomb was about to explode. He started running with the bomb around his stomach and only his underwear on. Juni ran as hard as he could to keep up with him. The security had pulled away the moment they saw a ticking bomb. They pretended to be running but preferred to let Juni be the frontrunner. Juni kept telling himself, 'I am running to the Italian restaurant and the lasagne is about to finish,' till they reached a lonely spot at the end of the lane with a little plank bridge and a wide river flowing under it. Juni thought of throwing the man into the river and letting the bomb explode, but the man was crying pitifully by now. He seemed to have some information that might be useful so it did not serve Juni's purpose to throw him into the water.

Juni tried to crack the password to diffuse the bomb. He tried suspect names like DORMETH, VIP, KILL, ASSASSIN, JUNI, but the bomb kept ticking and only a minute was left. Juni was wondering what to do when suddenly he remembered the poem. He entered PRAWN and the ticker stopped. The lock which secured the chain around the man snapped open. The man was crying like a baby and thanking him. Juni looked at him and asked, 'Who is behind this?'

'I don't know, sir. I was simply going to office when some hooded men picked me up and put me in their van. They tied the bomb to me. Then they dropped me near the meeting and told me to keep walking around or they would press the remote.'

'Did you notice anything that might help us track them down?' The man was still trembling. He could not remember anything. 'Okay, do me a favour and close your eyes,' said Juni.

The man did so.

'Picture yourself in the scene, and imagine someone coming at you. Who might it be? Does anything seem odd?'

'Pink and blue.'

'Come again?'

'A person passed me twice, around the block, wearing a pink and blue t-shirt while I was approaching the hall.'

'Anything else?'

'Yeah, he was wearing a strange perfume. It was ladies' perfume. He had an elephant-tusk pendant and a turban.'

Now, Juni thought that the man was probably hallucinating or thinking incoherently because of the incident.

Juni left him and re-entered the hall. The mayor, Monroe and Cameron were waiting for him. Cameron asked, 'So?' to which he replied, 'Just 49.5 seconds to spare.'

He told the mayor not to pull any more stunts like this, and then headed towards mayor's four bodyguards, but now there were only three. 'Obviously,' said Juni, rolling his eyes. He asked the three bodyguards about their missing companion, but they said that he was very ill. 'Of course,' said Juni in frustration again.

Juni, Cameron and Monroe came home dead tired.

'Let's have a pyjama party,' said Juni. There were enough bedrooms in the cottage to accommodate them all. They talked well into the night and then slept. They took the next day off even though they felt guilty. But they needed that break. They decided to have some nice sandwiches. Monroe went off as he had some 'personal errands' to take care of.

'I didn't think men did those,' said Dagger.

'What do you mean?' asked Cameron.

'Well, men don't have personal errands, for heaven's sake.'

'He may have someone he wants to meet in town,' said Cameron.

'Then why did he use the word "errand"?'

'Don't you have anything better to talk about?' asked Cameron.

'A study showed that women like talking more than men, so you tell me.'

'Are you married?' asked Cameron.

'Yes.'

'Then why didn't you say that the last time I asked?'

'If you ask the question twice, the answer usually doesn't change.'

'Then why did you change the answer?'

'Oh, God! Why are you so inquisitive?'

'Why are you being inquisitive and asking me if I am inquisitive? Are you trying to flirt with me?'

'I don't know, how do you define flirting?'

'The pre-seduction before the seduction.'

'In that case, "no"', grinned Juni.

'When might it have been a "yes"?'

'When you defined flirting as defined in the Oxford English Dictionary.'

As much as they wanted to talk and spend more time together, they couldn't not talk about the case. Cameron asked Juni if he had included those people who loved prawn on his list of suspects. Dagger was amused and said, 'No.'

Cameron then took Dagger to the Prawn Shack to ask the manager to give them the names of all the people who were their regular customers. The manager, Mr Ilaver Humphrey, was very dark and a unique mix of French and Indian parentage. He served an equally varied cuisine: from Indian prawn curry to prawn pakoras to prawn tempura and crackers. He was quick to oblige and respond. Juni asked him about the people who visited his shop, and he said he could get a list ready in less than a week, but Juni interjected and told him to take a full week. Juni never liked work done in a hurry, as that always increased the scope for error.

Juni and Cameron started walking around aimlessly. Juni was thinking of discussing the latest developments, but Cameron suddenly pulled him into an alley and told him that someone was following them. Juni replied calmly that he knew. After all, what good is a detective if he doesn't notice these things?

He went over the chain of possible actions he could take. He thought of jabbing the stalker but then wanted to make it quicker so he slowed down his pace, told Cameron not to say or do anything and then spun around and pushed the stalker's leg to the side. The stalker lost balance, then Juni put his head in a lock, and was ready to break his neck. He shouted, 'Cameron up front,' and she spun and tackled another attacker who had appeared out of nowhere. The second attacker, seeing that his partner was at a disadvantage, slipped out of Cameron's grip and ran away. 'Whoa!' Juni exclaimed. Cameron bowed and asked Dagger to talk to the stalker.

Dagger said, 'This girl here can cause you tremendous pain.'

The stalker was about to say something when Cameron interrupted and said, 'This girl? Come on, give me some credit.'

'So what do you want me to call you: my companion, assistant, girlfriend, Wife? What?'

'Never mind,' said Cameron.

Dagger continued and said, 'My girlfriend here can cause you some serious pain.' Cameron blushed a little but the blushing was followed by a hard kick to the gut of the man. 'That ought to cause excruciating pain.'

'You didn't even ask me the questions and kicked me without any reason!' the stalker shouted.

Dagger asked, 'Who sent you?'

He started to say 'Mmm…'

Juni said 'Yes say it!'

The assailant said, 'Mmmmmm scared, I can't breathe.' He put his hand near his neck and made a choking sound. Suddenly he bit the tablet on his neck piece, which had been hidden from sight. He started frothing at the mouth, writhed in pain and in a few seconds he was dead.

Dagger was very angry. Why did he keep forgetting about the neck piece? The man had given them no information.

When they got home, they found that Monroe had not yet returned from his errand. Cameron and Dagger were amazed at how long a 'personal errand' could last. Cameron stepped out for some time, and returned with a suitcase.

'What is this?' asked Dagger.

'I am going to live here till the case is solved,' she said.

'I don't even know you well enough for you to be staying with me,' said Dagger.

Cameron said, 'What do you want to know?'

'What is your surname?' asked Dagger.

She looked down and said, 'I don't know.'

'Why?'

Cameron sat down with a cup of coffee and started telling him the story of her life, 'I was born and raised in a little village in Japan. My mother died at my birth and my dad was killed by rich landlords.'

'I'm sorry.'

'I was adopted by the Sankyotsu temple monks, who raised me. I never had a name. Everybody called me "xiao", which means "little one". I was taught to fight. I was good at it and so the monks decided to put me in a special class for combat training. I was educated and also trained in kung-fu. Then, one day, they just let me go and said, "Go! Chase your dreams." They gave me some money. I tried to tell them that I had no dreams; I just wanted to live as an orphan in their monastery, but they shut the temple doors.

'I did not know what to do. I got a job in India, but don't ask me how I reached. I worked at a port; transported goods, keep accounts and made sure that they were in the right place. Then I decided that I would travel the world but a big company hired me; thanks to a lucky break. So, I got to work at one of the leading industrial houses. I was making money and I could afford a house and decent meals. Till I was about twenty years, I saved to buy a house, but in the end, I didn't do it, neither did I eat decent meals. I was wandering and searching for something that eluded me. Am I talking too much about myself?'

'No you are speaking freely.' Juni was staring at Cameron now.

'So I saved money and then one day I had a dream of becoming a detective. So I set out for unknown lands and came here. This is the perfect place. It's India, a place I am familiar with, and yet not India. I mean, staying here you are not really in India, are you? It's like a nowhere land nestled in India. I hope that I am making sense…like gorging on pies, shawarmas while knowing that paranthas and samosas are not too far away; that you can get them when you want to. And I am working with you, something that I really wanted to do.'

'Yes, I totally get where you are coming from! So you knew that you would work with me?' asked Dagger.

'When I came here, I got to know that you were working on a case and that night, I came to your place on purpose.'

'I am not too fond of Indian food, for your information. And I hope that you know that till the mayor pays you, you have to manage on your own,' said Juni.

At this Cameron laughed and said, 'Each person or assassin we catch, I flick the money from his wallet before you even get your hands on it.'

'Wow, I have been missing so much.'

'And also when we solve the case, you will remind the mayor to pay me…'

'What makes you think that?' Juni teased.

'I have learnt quite a few tricks,' she winked.

'You won't be needing them.'

Cameron blushed and asked, 'What's your backstory?'

'Almost the same as yours. My parents died young and I was raised in an orphanage. I ran away and then became a detective.' Juni was in no mood to talk about himself. He looked around.

'Where's Monroe?'

'I don't know!'

Just then Monroe walked in. Dagger said, 'What took you so long?'

'Oh, nothing! Just caught in a big stampede.'

'Oh, someone doesn't know how to lie. What was your personal errand?'

'If I told you, it would not be personal.'

Chapter Eight

The next day, no one complained about being tired. They all got to work.

'Every day we sit down with a cup of coffee and "work" but we do not come to a conclusion,' said Monroe. 'What are we supposed to work on?'

'Here, work on the suspect list,' said Dagger

He drew out the updated list. Together, they scoured it, then spent the next few days going over the crime scenes, and all the bullets they'd gathered, until they finally found a pattern. The snipers had been identified by Inspector Singh. And a startling fact came to light after the results of the autopsies came out. All the snipers had been suffering from terminal diseases and were about to die.

'Why would the killer employ these people?' asked Cameron.

'I don't know' said Juni dismissively.

Monroe said, 'Maybe he wanted people who had no hope and would embrace death readily if they were caught. No wonder, we have been unable to catch a single one alive. They don't want to live. They would rather die than be subjected to a long and painful death.'

Dagger said that the next time they caught an assassin they would cut off his neck piece.

He also pointed out that now the dates of the attacks were completely random. Something had happened along the way that had made the killer change his mind about the pattern. The killer had access to what they were talking about. They had not followed their own rule of not discussing the case in the house. There could be more microphones hidden in the house that they hadn't yet discovered.

Juni and Cameron started piecing all the inferences together. Cameron said, 'Let's call the killer "Veron", for convenience sake.' Juni was amused, 'Why "Veron" of all the names?' Cameron said, 'Oh! Just an oblique opposite to hero with an "n" added to make it more musical!' Juny grinned and agreed. They now knew that 'Veron' could speak Russian, had the letters M and Y or V in his name, and was probably wealthy since he had been able to hire so many assassins. The team made a final draft of the list of suspects, but it was still not a short one.

Funnily, Mr Crow also was on it. His name was Maynard Crow, but they had to check if he knew Russian. Juni suggested that they take a break and go to the Shawarma Point.

'Don't you have anything else to eat? All that goes on in your life is shawarmas and pies!' said Cameron.

But they still ended up at the Shawarma Point. Juni said, 'Darling, food is of two types, one of them is heaven and the other type is umm…' He took a bite of his shawarma and stopped. Cameron rolled her eyes and ordered a salad.

Suddenly a man came and bumped into Monroe. He dropped a tissue. There was some text written on it. Dagger snatched it from Monroe and his eyes widened in horror. He got up and ran towards the stranger. Cameron watched them curiously, but they disappeared.

Finally, Juni returned sweating and out of breath, looking furious. Cameron asked what had happened, to which he said that there were curses written on the paper, and that he had been called a knobhead. Cameron was bemused. 'So, being called a knobhead will make you run… What an ego!'

Dagger said, 'Look, this may be an idyllic place for you but it's getting to me. Anyway, let's get on with our food.'

They thought of ordering a pitcher of beer but Monroe objected. Instead, they ordered only three glasses. On the way back, they were not high and could easily stay vigilant. They stood for some time in the garden taking in the fresh scented air and reviewed the day's happenings. On a sombre note, they retired for the night.

The next day, they woke up to find that a letter had arrived from Mr Humphrey, the Prawn Shack manager. It contained the list of prawn-lovers. They looked at the list, and added the common names from the earlier list to a new one.

Suddenly, Juni sat bolt upright. In the list of eight, six were already dead and two had left town. It was a bizarre coincidence, but Juni did not believe in those. A coincidence was a coincidence only till the vital connections between the events hadn't been understood. Once they were solved, then, like a jigsaw puzzle, the coincidence disappeared and became part of the chain of cause and effect.

The detectives went to the restaurants and met Mr Humphrey. They told him to never send any information by post. Then they asked Mr Humphrey the whereabouts of the two people who had left town. Mr Humphrey was clueless. He asked why they wanted to know, but Dagger refused to elaborate on the matter.

The three then headed towards the port to find out more about the people who had left town in the last week. They also told the port official not to let any more people leave town without informing Juni. There were many objections over this harsh decision but they had to continue their investigation and were ready to enact such harsh policies.

Dagger knew he was very lucky to have such trustworthy friends to help him, so he decided to give them a surprise. Since he could not think of one, he let the idea slide.

'Can we all eat le poulet roti tonight?' asked Monroe.

'Poult roast? What?' asked Dagger to which Monroe replied, 'I will cook tonight and then I need to go on leave tomorrow.' Juni agreed.

They ate the *poulet roti* and loved it, but they preferred cheap take-out shawarma to gourmet food which was available in such small portions. Juni could never figure out why such food was dished out in such small quantities.

Juni and Cameron decided to go over the suspect list once more and also thought of paying another visit to the port. Then, they made yet another list, which had the names of the common people from the original list and the port list. Next, they made another list with the common people of the list with the prawn-shack list and the port list. By this time the work was getting pretty complicated, so they took some time to understand where exactly they had reached. All three decided to take a walk. Juni was looking at how sleepy the eating joints looked in the dead of the night. He felt a little sad at seeing them so woebegone. No delectable smells, no people merrily talking and eating! The saddest scene was this—an eating place closed and desolate. And add to that the dark, cold night and you had the perfect recipe for feeling low.

The next day, they decided to visit the mayor and update him on their findings. They went to his residence.

'Who might this beautiful lady be? I happen to have seen her earlier also and have been waiting for an introduction.' the mayor asked on seeing Cameron.

'This is Cameron,' Dagger said. 'My assistant.'

'Yes, I have seen her around. What happened to the other assistant?'

'Oh! Monroe? He is on leave.'

'So you must be paying her, yes?'

'No! I believe that is your job!'

'Any updates on the case?'

'That's what we're here for.'

They gave him all the information they had.

The mayor did not seem to be impressed. 'Why don't you talk to Randy? See if he's got any leads,' he said.

Juni was reluctant, but then he remembered that he had seen Randy at the arms shop. He obviously knew a lot about the case. In fact, he might even be half a step ahead of him. Some help would be welcome.

He decided to go to Randy's office. As he entered, Randy said, 'Ah, you took a long time.' Ignoring him, Juni asked if he had got anything new to work with to which he replied with a wicked glint, 'Maybe. I have cracked the code.'

'Whaat!' exclaimed Juni.

'Yes! I have, indeed, cracked the code and come up with the key to understanding it,' said Randy.

'Wait! How the hell did you get the numbers in the first place? I did not give the exact numbers to the mayor.'

I took your notepad and noticed a torn page, then I shaded the page behind the torn one and viola, the numbers were visible!' exclaimed Randy in an excited tone.

'Ohh, you dumb idiot!' said Juni in a pitiful tone.

'What?' said Randy, who had expected a different response to his genius. He moved his hand nervously to his ear. His grey hair looked like it desperately needed combing.

'Let me guess, if the original number is greater than 15, it is halved, and if it is lower than 15 the number is left as it is, and in the pattern the supposed killer left, all the original numbers were the dates of the murders, right?'

'Yes,' said Randy.

'The paper you traced wasn't the one with the numbers,' declared Juni.

'Well, then, what was it?' asked Randy.

Juni, now on his way out, said, 'It's a formula that my team and I use to decide the number of fish fingers we can eat after a murder. They are really stress-busting, you know.'

Randy was agitated. 'If you wanted to mislead me then at least you could have done it more cleverly,' he said.

Juni muttered, 'Damn! Does this fellow leave nothing?' He turned back and said to him, 'By the way, it's "PRISM"!'

'What?' asked Randy.

'Four down, five letters, Cupid ties a bow in the sky,' said Juni.

Randy gaped at him and turned back to his crossword. '"Prism" fits perfectly,' Randy thought, '*This man had brains after all.*' He looked at Juni with new respect. Juni nonchalantly turned and walked out. He was hungry!

That evening, Juni and Cameron decided to go to the pie restaurant. They drank and ate and ate. They had a long argument over whether shawarmas were better or pies. They grew more and more garrulous and then, realizing their foolishness, got into a gregarious mood. As they were walking,

Cameron was singing a silly tune and Juni thought that he saw a shadow. His ears perked and in a moment his tipsiness vanished. He told Cameron in a whisper that somebody could be following them. They looked around, and suddenly all was quiet. There was no movement. Juni sighed and turned. And there, at the Shawarma Point, he saw Monroe eating. He cursed him for experiencing heaven without them.

The next morning, Cameron came down from her room to find Juni looking totally exhausted. He did not seem to have slept at all. '*Detective work is always romanticized. It is more file work than fieldwork,*' he thought. He got up and stretched. Then he told Cameron to get ready.

Cameron put on her jeans and canvas shoes and tied her signature ponytail. Jeans were the new fashion statement across the world. As Meraupatnam was a port town with many nationalities cohabiting, the latest trends were more accessible here. In a patterned shirt and blue jeans, she looked like an innocent schoolgirl, but one look at her eyes and you would know that she was not to be fooled with. Her eyes were steady and had the hardness of experience behind them. Not big, but shining with knowledge and sometimes humour, but mostly glinting with cynicism.

Juni was looking very suave in his business suit, but his mouth was pressed into a thin line of grim anger and worry. Cameron moved towards the garden gate and suddenly turned back and came in with a letter. She looked puzzled. The envelope was marked 'confidential' and addressed to Juni.

There was another paper inside which had the same poem that he had read earlier, and an audio tape. Juni was quite taken aback. He knew that someone was trying to help him but he was very perplexed about who it could be.

They went back inside and connected the cassette into a tape recorder. They were shocked at what they heard. There were audio clips of all their important conversations. There was an audio clip of the assassin getting beaten up by Veron because he was resistant towards Veron's policy of using and killing. When Juni played the third audio track, an ominous voice filled the room.

'I am he who is in the service to my master. I am at the end of my life and find that I have been misled and duped. Christ have mercy on me. I repent, and helping you is part of my penance. Lord have mercy. I have made many important discoveries in this case and I am supporting you. I have cancer and am going to die soon. The Master gave me money for the protection of my family after my death and so I agreed to do this job.

'All that I know is that the Master is a person who stays close to you. He can hear all your conversations. But he is not the Master—the Supreme Lord is the one above. The tyrant is a merciless tyrant—a user. But when I met the tyrant, he was in a mask. But I can say that I smelt a sweet perfume emanating from him. My mind is wandering. May God be with you.'

There was bile rising in Juni's throat. He was shit scared and decided to talk only in public even though he could not see any microphones in his house.

They started discussing the case at the Shawarma Point or at the pie restaurant. The case now gave them a new culinary satisfaction. They were eager to discuss it as it meant more of heaven. Their guilt over binging was also assuaged as they were having what they called a 'working lunch' or a 'working supper.' Soon, Juni found that the trousers that used to hang so smartly on his frame were getting a little uncomfortable. He looked down and saw a hint of a belly straining at the trouser button. He was shaken. He had to do something about it. He had taken his fitness for granted, he mused. He had to cut down on his food. Taking the hint, he started going for long walks and jogs in the park.

Chapter Nine

One day, after returning from the park, Juni was heading in for a bath as his t-shirt was sticking uncomfortably to him. Monroe came and cut him off in a huff and said, 'But I need to use the washroom for a minute.' Without waiting for a reply, he rushed in.

Juni sat on the edge of the sofa, careful not to let his wet t-shirt touch the back. Cameron came in looking as fit and svelte as ever. 'How do you eat so much and still maintain that body?' asked Juni.

'I work out.'

'How? I have never seen you exercise or go to the park for a jog.'

'Of course, I work out—I am a ninja...almost.'

'Ohhh!' Juni and Cameron heard a scream.

'Fire!' screamed Monroe and ran out of the bathroom.

Juni went in with a fire extinguisher and contained

the flames. Then he came down and asked Monroe how this stupid accident had taken place. Monroe said that he had been playing with a hair dryer and then something happened. 'Wait! What? Why were you playing with a hair dryer?' Monroe blushed. Cameron laughed and the issue was forgotten.

Juni went for a bath and took an unusually long time. By the time he came out, his teammates were fast asleep, sprawled on the sofas and settees in the living room. He looked at Cameron for a moment and almost instantaneously, Cameron looked up at him and smiled. Juni was a little scared but then he asked, 'How did you know that I was looking at you?'

'I'm a Ninja,' she exclaimed lazily. Juni didn't say another word and hit the sack.

The next morning, they didn't do much except lie around at home trying to sort through some paperwork. They ate normal food the whole day, but tanked themselves up with beer at night. 'Don't get too loaded,' said Monroe, but Juni said, 'I'm fifty-seven and that's all I do!' This made Cameron and Monroe burst into laughter but Cameron also realized that he was intoxicated so they made him sleep and called it a night themselves.

Cameron was up early the next morning but Juni and Monroe didn't wake up until noon.

'What time did you get up?' asked Juni.

'About 7 a.m.,' replied Cameron

'Don't ninjas get hangovers?'

'Why do you drink so much?'

'You drink for pleasure. I drink to die.'

She winked and continued doing whatever the hell she was doing. Then he looked again carefully. She seemed to be doing some strange, ninja stretches. Then she asked, 'You are fifty-seven?'

'No,' Juni replied, 'When did I say that?'

'Never mind… So, how old are you?'

'I'm twenty-seven.'

'Okay.'

Monroe walked in.

'Where were you?' Juni asked.

He said, 'Looking for a reason.'

'What?'

'Nothing.'

Cameron and Juni walked to a café to get some coffee.

Since there had been no activity over the past few days, they thought that perhaps Veron had stopped planning further.

They finished and since there was no waiter in sight, they decided to pay the cashier. As they settled the bill, Juni was growing nostalgic about his past adventures with payment, and almost instantaneously, Cameron spun around and took out her gun from her not-so-high boots. She shot straight up onto the balcony of an old church. Juni ran up to the spot and searched for the shooter but found no one. He came back to Cameron and asked why she had done it. She calmly but sternly replied, 'Veron has stepped up his game.'

'Why do you say that?'

Cameron told Juni that a bullet fired at them had fallen midway. This seemed impossible but then Dagger saw that there were two bullets fused together on the ground as though they had collided mid-air. He spun around and asked Cameron how she had done this impossible task.

She replied, 'Cause I'm a ninja!'

Juni just ignored it and rolled his eyes.

They searched the balcony of the old church, but didn't find much—just a piece of cloth which was obviously from a coat. Its colour was serene blue. As Cameron turned around to leave, Dagger saw something quite unusual. There was a mark of gunpowder on the balcony railing, and an unmistakably familiar scent. He tried to sniff deeply and Cameron had an irrepressible urge to giggle at seeing him wrinkling his nose and then his brows.

The next day, Juni was thinking about the scent, and decided to go to the market in search of something—tuna sandwiches! They went to the Prawn Shack. There were hardly any people around. It seemed to be a lonely little place. The manager Humphrey was nowhere to be seen.

After finishing the sandwich, Juni picked a rose from the vase on the table and went to the lady in a frothy green dress who was standing uncertainly at the door, wondering whether to come in or not. He presented the rose to her. She looked delighted. Next, he invited her to his table and said that he needed to use the washroom. And yes, he disappeared, leaving the lady with a rose in one hand and a cheque in the other.

The lady in a frothy green dress rushed out and looked for Juni when a stranger shouted, 'Dagger strikes again, people!'

'Wait till Mr Crow hears of this.' A little crowd had gathered. The lady was sweating and shouting in anger and shaking her fist at where Juni had disappeared. The people who had gathered smirked and talked about the capabilities of Juni. He had become famous in the town of Meraupatnam.

Juni had escaped the lady's ire. He thought that people were now seeing him more as a prankster than a detective. He felt a renewed urgency as it seemed that his reputation was at stake. Something about the scent was troubling him but he could not figure out what it was.

When he reached the little cottage, he saw Cameron standing outside shouting like a hysterical wife, 'You cheated on me! That's just rotten. You know I love tuna sandwiches but you went alone and I thought that we had a pact that we would do everything together!'

Juni grinned and teased, 'Yes, in all dangers and life-threatening situations, not in the pleasures!'

Cameron said, 'Well, I take my tuna sandwiches seriously and I guess you are willing to trade a ninja for a tuna. Let me pack and be gone.'

Juni decided that he had better pacify her so he said, 'Here, I got some packed for you,' and winked at her. 'Since we have a new pact to share everything, I don't mind sharing a part of the tuna sandwich!'

Cameron gave him a light slap and told him not to push his luck. Then feeling satiated and happy, they decided to go for a walk. As they were strolling and looking around, Cameron asked him where she could buy some of her ninja equipment.

Juni was trying to think of an answer when a voice hailed them: 'Whoa, there!' They turned around and saw Randy.

Juni grinned, 'Let's see if he can help! How are you, Randy?'

Randy was thrilled at being greeted by Juni. 'How are your investigations going?'

Juni said, 'I may need some help from you after all…'

Randy was perspiring and he was feverishly rubbing his ear. He was excited. 'Yes, tell me, tell me!'

'Well, Cameron here needs some ninja equipment. Where can we get it?'

Randy beamed, 'You have come to the right person. I know just the person who can help you. He is a loner and will not talk to anyone. In fact, the town has almost forgotten him. His name is Mr Wong.'

Cameron was surprised, 'But how are you his friend?'

Randy blushed, 'Oh, we play chess sometimes, and I offered to help his daughter with her exams.'

Randy was looking very awkward. He was staring at the ground.

Juni winked at Cameron and laughed, 'Well, well ... Who would have thought? And what's her name?'

'Chuki,' replied Randy. 'They are from Manipur and have been settled here for the last decade or so.'

'Can you take us there?' asked Juni.

Randy said that it would not be possible. Mr Wong was a recluse and met no one. He would pack up and leave if he knew that people were becoming so intrusive. Cameron gave him a list of all the things she wanted and some money.

Randy was extremely happy to be a part of Juni's investigations. He said, 'I will do this and I hope you will also take me with you on missions.'

Juni gave a non-committal answer but that was enough for Randy. He said excitedly, 'I think that these sudden attacks were not done in a particular order I think that the killer who you call Veron may be working on other things, so that explains the gaps and intervals before each killing.'

Juni said, 'Well deduced Randy.' They said bye to Randy and made their way back to the cottage.

Days and weeks went by but there were no more murders. Just once there was the sound of the crack of the bullet and as the people and Juni rushed towards it, they discovered that it was a false alarm. A huge crate had fallen from a crane onto the ground and made a loud sound. So, their theory that Veron was a busy man seemed to be true. Juni tried to read his mind. He seemed to be an extremely clever, manipulative and cruel person who might have a psychological problem of deriving pleasure from controlling and killing people. Perhaps this person had had an unhappy childhood and been subjected to a lot of bullying and physical abuse. But what was his motive? Revenge, money or just a diseased mind—or a combination of all three? All this thinking had made Juni very hungry. So, he decided to take a break. He put on his overcoat as there was a slight chill in the air and set off for the by-now familiar and endearing cobbled lanes of the somnolent and sinister town to look for a nice café.

Chapter Ten

The equipment from Mr Wong finally arrived one morning. Cameron was very excited. She opened it with Juni. She picked up her new throwing stars and screamed with happiness, and spent the rest of the day obsessing over her new items.

Days were passing and nothing earth-shatteringly consequential was happening with their investigations. Mr Crow was becoming more and more obnoxious. One morning Juni and Cameron told Monroe that they were going to meet Mr Crow to 'fix' him. As they walked down the road that housed the Prawn Shack, the manager waved at them and they reciprocated. Juni wanted to stop but Cameron would have none of it. Suddenly, Cameron moved like lightning. She spun and threw a star and there was the sound of a crunch. Dagger realized that the shuriken had blasted a huge rock that had been flung at them.

'Zounds! Holy Shit! What in the name of Lord Jesus was that!' screamed Juni, jumping like a toad.

Cameron's eyes twinkled as she said, 'I'm a ninja.'

'But still, how did you get the star-like thing…'

'Shuriken,' corrected Cameron.

'Yes, shrimpiken, right in the middle of this stone?'

'It's shuriken, can't you think of anything besides food?'

'But how are you so accurate?'

'It's the same reason you can shoot a bull's eye.'

Juni was stunned and didn't say anything, just continued walking. They were getting more and more unpopular. They decided to turn back and head homewards.

At home, Juni was coming out of the washroom when he saw Cameron's equipment. Curious, he picked up a shuriken and the point pricked his finger. He started bleeding.

'Zounds, what the damn hell is this?'

Cameron turned and replied, 'It's one of the deadliest shurikens in the world. And don't touch my stuff! Some of those tips are poisonous! You could have died.'

Juni just backed away with a petrified expression. He never touched Cameron's equipment again.

Later that day, the mayor visited them. He was wearing a suede coat and charcoal pants. He was the mayor after all! A gold chain discreetly pointed to an expensive watch in his upper pocket. The mayor asked Juni about Monroe, 'I have hired him as your assistant and yet he never seems to be around.'

Juni fibbed that Monroe had not been well for the past few weeks. And then Juni pointed towards Cameron and said, 'She is very efficient and working very hard. She saved three people recently.' Juni looked back at Cameron, who was walking towards the kitchen to call Monroe. She blushed. Monroe came out of the kitchen and exchanged a few pleasantries with the mayor. Then, the mayor left and Juni, Monroe and Cameron sat in the living room. They spent the next few hours pouring over the reports and trying to come up with viable theories. By the time they finished, it was dark. After having a quick meal, they retreated to their rooms in easy camaraderie. They had become used to each other; they would eat together, talk together, sleep together…in separate rooms, but under one roof. They would go on food adventures and look for little shops where they could experience new culinary delights.

The next day, Juni, Cameron and Monroe found a little eatery which had some unique dishes, including an Indian Balti pie! Whoever had heard of something like that—a pie made in a little Indian bucket with just a hint of spices? The restaurant was on the first floor. They climbed up the stairs. It was a cosy little place. At the far end of the room, there was a bamboo trellis with a flower vine looking very pretty leading to a balcony beyond. The trio went inside and was soon eating the pie.

Juni felt a pricking sensation on his back as if a pair of eyes were piercing into him. He turned around but saw no one. He went back to his food but made a silent gesture to

Cameron. Now, they were very vigilant. There were very few people in the little eatery, only another a couple and a person immersed in his newspaper. Suddenly, Juni turned and stared at the newspaper, and very slowly, a pair of eyes peered over it. As soon as they saw Juni staring, they retreated quickly behind the newspaper.

Juni decided to take the bull by its horns. He quietly and quickly made a move towards the man and snatched the newspaper away. The man behind was Randy. Juni was annoyed.

'What are you doing here?'

'Why? What are you doing here?' asked Randy, twitching nervously.

'I am eating Balti pie.'

'I am going to order Balti pie.'

'Oh, don't be a smart aleck.'

'No, you are the smart aleck. Look, why don't we work together. I thought that we were friends. I got the equipment from Mr Wong and you solved my crossword. I thought that I could really help you with the investigation.'

'Okay! But I don't like being hounded. What do you know? Out with it.'

'There is a definite link to prawn.'

'Yeah! Thanks for the great input!' smirked Juni.

'And what do you know apart from the long lists of suspects that you keep editing?'

Now, Juni was irritated and was about to say something

when Randy screamed looking at the balcony, 'Watch out!'

Monroe was screaming in excruciating pain. Before Dagger realized what had happened, a sniper spun around and jumped down from the balcony on the street below. When Juni looked over the railing, he looked down and saw the sniper writhing in pain. There was a shrimpikin in his crotch. Cameron had brought him down and how!

'Seriously?' shouted Juni, as they made their way down.

'What?' asked Cameron with a mischievous smile. They reached the spot within seconds. He was still groaning in agony.

'Who are you?' Juni demanded of the sniper.

'My name is Veron.'

Juni and Cameron looked at each other in shock and disbelief. 'Who employed you?'

Instead of replying, the sniper screamed.

Dagger sensed an urgency and asked him again, 'What's happening? Why are you in pain? Have you taken a pill?'

This time Veron said, 'The riddle that you received... refer to it!'

Accuse him; well, you could be shot!
Catch him; impossible it is!
Only if you find evidence and witnesses, can you not be
considered a pawn!
In this treachery by the lover of prawn; prawns do not
live in old factories, my dear
They require water everywhere...

Before the sniper could say anything more, his head fell back and he was dead.

Once more, Juni was taken aback. Two lines had been added to the riddle. 'Prawns didn't live in factories!' Randy was standing beside them and his hand was twitching and pulling his left ear compulsively. Juni shouted at him. 'Get out! What are you doing standing here? Get out!' Randy almost skipped out, muttering the riddle to himself.

Monroe was rushed to the hospital. He had hurt his leg and might have to be in the hospital for some time. Now, Juni and Cameron were on their own.

The killer had given them another clue. Factory, why had he mentioned a factory? Juni decided to investigate all the factories around the town. He took out a map of the town and tried to see if there were any abandoned factories in the area. They found one. It did not seem to be too far away. Juni and Cameron decided to walk there. Juni marked the location on his map. It was about a mile from the town, but in a hilly and desolate area. There was no proper road. Creepers and wild growth had invaded the road that once led to the factory. It looked like a place fit for ghosts. Cameron looked a little uncomfortable.

Juni grinned, 'Don't tell me that you are getting spooked.' Cameron gave a stern look. 'This is no time to joke. I think someone is behind us.'

Juni said, 'It's a ghost from the haunted maison near the factory.'

Cameron told him to shut up. Suddenly there was a movement behind the tree. Both Juni and Cameron turned and hid behind a broken wall. It was eerily silent. Juni took a pebble and threw it at the tree; there was a loud yelp and a dog came running out. And so did another shadow. They collided and there was another scream. It was Randy! Both the dog and Randy were rolling on the ground. Juni suppressed his laughter and separated the two. Randy was shivering and clutching Cameron as if his life depended on it. The dog was yelping. Juni recognized the dog as the town stray. 'Come here, Buddy! What are you doing here?' he said, fondling its ears. 'Mr Randy, for an investigator, you create a lot of ruckus.'

Randy was clutching his ears in agitation. 'I thought it was a ghost! Otherwise, I would have been as silent as a kitten.'

Juni said wryly, 'Yeah, a big furry brown ghost. To be an investigator, you need both brains and nerves. Or you say bye to your life.' Randy looked embarrassed and walked away.

Cameron looked at Randy with pity. Juni told her to move on and stop feeling bad for the weird little loner. But something flickered on Juni's face.

He and Cameron went near the factory and he pointed at the crushed foliage and grass nearby. 'The ghosts certainly do come alive at night. There is some activity happening here. That's why, Buddy, the dog was also here. He may be getting leftover food. And the grass tells its own story.'

They decided that they would come at night for, at that time, the ghosts would surely be up and about. They had to be properly armed. The walk had made them ravenous. They went for lunch to the pie restaurant.

After lunch, they thought of going to the police station and meeting Inspector Singh and keeping him up to date with the field mission.

'Hey, Juni! How is it going? Any breakthrough yet?' With each word that the inspector spoke, his jewellery sparkled.

Juni, desperately trying to ignore the sight, said, 'Yes, we are working on it but at this stage, we need your help. We need some equipment as matters are heating up.' Singh was very supportive. He took Juni to the armoury. 'Just fill up a requisition form and take what you want,' he said. There was a mind-boggling array of weapons—handguns, grenades, rifles, sniper guns, semi-automatic guns and automatic guns.

It was all there; Juni picked them up like a child picks candies. But Cameron just stood there. 'Don't you need weapons?' asked the inspector, his thick beard moving up and down and his eyes crinkling indulgently.

'No, I have my own.'

'Little girls shouldn't handle dangerous things,' the inspector said.

'Seriously?' said Juni, 'You are going to use those little metal stars?'

She threw two at Juni. They pinned him to the wall. He was irritated because he couldn't do much except stay still. Cameron laughed at his discomfiture and took the cash in his pockets before she released him. The inspector was taken aback. He couldn't believe that this innocent-looking girl could overpower a man twice her size. 'Bravo!' he said, and patted Cameron, wiggling his tongue vigorously, revealing his tongue piercing. Scared at the sight, Cameron took two steps back. 'Pleasure to meet you, pleasure to meet you,' said the inspector and chuckled at the immobile Juni. He was looking very grumpy.

Cameron laughed, 'Nothing hurt except your pride, my friend. Now, you will avoid the fall.'

Juni looked rather annoyed and then grudgingly smiled and soon they were friends again.

As the night drew closer, they took out their weapons and decided which ones to use. Juni chose two basic semi-automatic handguns. He then took a rifle for his main weapon and chose a machine gun for his secondary one. He loaded his belt with grenades and smoke bombs.

Cameron picked up a set of shurikens for emergency use and two sets of throwing spikes for normal use, and herself as the main weapon. Juni laughed at seeing this but before he realized it, he was on the ground and Cameron was pinning him. She twisted and Dagger felt unbearable pain, which was gone when she moved. She then said, 'You don't learn your lessons, do you? Never underestimate.'

Juni grinned and said, 'No, no, I learn my lessons quite fast, but then I also like to have you near me and for that, I am ready to suffer some starry pain.' Cameron was taken aback and blushed furiously. There was an awkward silence.

They still had a couple of hours to go before they went to the factory. Juni was very fidgety. Time just didn't seem to pass. Finally, Juni came up with an idea. There was a chess set lying in a corner of the living room. Juni and Cameron looked at each other and nodded. Soon they were immersed in a game. It was a draw, each person had only one piece left, their kings. 'Why should the king be the last to go? Why should he be protected at all costs? He is certainly not the most useful piece!' said Cameron.

'Because that is the way of the world,' said Juni.

'Even though the queen does all the work, is versatile and defends the king?'

'Yes!'

'And is more powerful than the king?'

'No, the queen may be stronger but she is not more powerful.'

'The king has the power. And sits on his fat ass, enjoying it and makes sacrifices of the rest of the pieces—his armies, his ministers, his queen!'

'As I said, "Way of the world".'

'Then it's a pity... No wonder, the world has so much conflict. Hard work and strength are not rewarded. It is an unjust world. Even Veron. Look how he is making pawns of the people to serve his own ends. He must have a lot of power.'

Juni looked at Cameron. 'Yes, you are right! He must be rich and powerful to be able to enslave so many people and make them commit murder.'

'Could it be the general, Humphrey or some other well-to-do person in the town? Could the killer be one of the Dormeth Lane residents?'

'What! A world, where the killer and killed live together!'

'Way of the world...'

Monroe was likely to be released from the hospital the next day. The injury had not been that serious as it was thought to be. They were looking forward to him being back, even though his leg would be in a cast.

Then, tired of so much discussion, they looked at the clock. It was approaching midnight. Time had flown! It was time to go!

Chapter Eleven

They were finally out of the house and heading towards the factory. As soon as they reached, they realized that there was something that they had not noticed: a railway line running behind the old factory. They entered the premises, and made their way to the main hall from where they could hear voices. It seemed that there were some people there. The main hall was like a central courtyard with interior railings along each floor interspersed with walls and windows, overlooking the main hall. They knew that Veron would not be so stupid as to have stayed in the factory. As Cameron was slimmer than Juni, she climbed up swiftly to the top floor through the network of windows, soundlessly, and looked around. It was a clear night but there was not enough moonlight to compensate for the dark. She disappeared from Juni's sight.

When she came back, she didn't say anything, just signalled to Juni to follow her. They reached a place where there was a perfect shooting perch, so he took out his sniper rifle. It was a small alcove at right angles to the railing completely hidden from view, overlooking the main hall where some nefarious activity seemed to be taking place. The scene was amazing. Five men were arranging all kinds of guns and weapons in cartons. A fat man was chewing something. His ruddy face looked menacing. He seemed to be issuing orders. Juni took his time and then aimed at the fat man with a tranquillizing dart.

Before anybody else turned around, Dagger quickly shot four more darts that went and hit four different people.

'Watch my back,' said Juni.

Cameron obeyed. Both had their weapons in hand.

As they went around the wall, Cameron tugged at Juni. He stopped. Cameron threw a star and they heard a scream of sheer pain. Juni was impressed. Cameron climbed up onto a window ledge. The ledge was only about six inches wide. Juni watched with bated breath. After a few steps, she dropped down and sat on the head of a gunman and swung his head in a Spanish wrestling move. He went crashing down, Juni shot him with a dart.

Juni sensed footsteps behind him. He spun around and smacked the head of his attacker with his rifle and tranquillized him.

Cameron said, 'We are finished here, let's go.'

'No,' said Juni. He shushed her and listened, then he closed his eyes and pointed his gun somewhere and shot it.

'AAargh!' came a scream.

'Now we are done.'

'Bu-but how did you do that?' asked Cameron.

'You're not the only one with exceptional skills here,' grinned Juni.

They called the police and handed the criminals to them.

The factory was now desolate. Suddenly, there came a whining sound. They turned around and saw that it was Buddy the dog.

'Oh, you poor little thing, you wanted your morsel, didn't you?' asked Cameron. She reached into her pocket and took out a packet of biscuits.

It was nearly morning. Juni and Cameron were famished. They decided to walk back to town to a nice breakfast place and from there went to the police station.

When all the people they had tranquillized had woken up, they saw that they were tied and in the police station. Juni asked Cameron if she wanted to ask questions first, but she said that Juni could go ahead. He went in and interrogated them. He did not get any answers, and neither did Cameron.

The criminals were extremely hardened and stubborn. The police had been working on them since the early hours of the morning, but they were having a very difficult time.

Meanwhile, Monroe was home from the hospital. His leg was in a soft bandage and he was using a crutch to walk. Juni looked at him and expressed his relief that it was just a hairline fracture and that he was sort of on his feet even though he would not be able to run. 'But you can make some nice stuff for us in the kitchen,' he said. Monroe looked upset but did not answer.

Some days passed with nothing significant happening. One day, Cameron and Dagger went out to get some provisions. Monroe whose leg was much better, went to the prison to meet the suspects. He returned in a huff and told Juni that they had managed to escape. One of them had arranged a pocket knife, which he kept hidden, and as soon as the guard came into the cell to deliver food, he caught hold of him and threatened to pierce his jugular, if he didn't give him the key.

Juni looked at Monroe, 'But why are you bleeding?'

'It happened when I was in the waiting room talking to the head of the police station. The criminals charged out and there was a scuffle. The fat fellow swung his knife and the guard's gun was in his other hand. His left- and right-hand coordination was not too great but he was very active for his weight, and as he was swinging wildly, my arm got a deep gash. *'Je Hugo Monroe n'a pas de muscle, je suis* a waste!'

Meanwhile, a local policeman came and gave Juni a piece of paper that they had found in the prison cell. On it was another message.

Catch Me If You Can Or Die While You Can.

A chill went down Juni's spine.

He didn't want to waste any more time, so instead of going to the Prawn Shack, he just had a sandwich at home. Then he turned his attention to the message. It was more like a threat than a puzzle. The mastermind was getting more and more brazen. He was playing with them. Meanwhile, Cameron was sharpening and counting her shurikens.

That night Cameron went to the market to get herself some formal paraphernalia. She saw a lovely little pizza place in a small alley. An American soldier who had fought in the war had finally settled in the little town. At the time he came to the town, pizza and doughnuts had become a craze in America. He had been told by the locals that it would not be available within a radius of a thousand miles at least. So, he decided to open a pizzeria. On returning home, she told Juni about it.

'Why don't we try the new pizzeria round the corner? Just for tonight, then we will eat healthy,' said Juni. Cameron readily agreed.

'So, Miss Mexican ninja…' said Juni.

'Please stop calling me that. For one thing, I know for sure that I am not Mexican. And your name, "Dagger"! Why the name Dagger? Or was it some other name? You are not from North India, are you? Oh! Wait a minute, are you Dagar, a North Indian Punjabi?' laughed Cameron.

'Do I look like one to you?' Juni asked, his eyes flashing.

Cameron looked at him. 'No. You look like you're from Central Asia.'

'Oh, you mean crossing the mountains and rivers with bare feet, facing the elements to reach here… Eh! What about

Germany?' Juni asked.

Cameron looked at him and said, 'Well, you could be, and then, you could be my Nordic king.'

Juni was quick to reply, 'Oh, your Nordic king. I like that.'

Cameron blushed slightly, laughed and turned away.

'Let's focus on our food.'

They finished their meal and then hit the sack.

Chapter Twelve

One week later, they discovered that they were still hooked to the lovely pizzeria. It was a nice place with climbers hanging on a trellis and rustic décor with some pots and pans, and other kitchen implements hanging aesthetically on the walls, which had a rough, stone finish. Cameron thought about how beautiful it looked...like a garden of paradise.

'Hey, Desmund,' said Dagger, signalling to the owner of the pizza place. He waved to him in response.

'I'll have my usual.'

'I've added bacon to your favourite meat pizza,' said Desmund.

'Exxecelleennt! Get me a full-sized pizza and a few chocolate doughnuts.'

'Okey dokey,' said Desmund.

'Oh! The mayor is expected here any minute. So make that two!'

The mayor arrived in a huff. 'Sorry, I am late.'

'Not to worry, you are only five minutes late,' said Juni.

The mayor said philosophically, 'Sometimes, five minutes make all the difference.'

Juni and Cameron were discussing the case with the mayor. He was congratulating them on the factory raid and also commented about the unfortunate escape of the prisoners. Then he asked Juni, 'Did you get any other clue?'

'Not really, but the prisoners did leave a message.'

'Oh! Did they? Can I take a look?'

'Yeah sure. As a matter of fact, I have it with me now.'

Juni took out the little piece of paper and handed it to the mayor. As he was about to read it, a waiter accidentally bumped into him and the paper dropped into a glass of water and the writing faded away. The mayor was furious. He held the waiter by the collar of his shirt.

Randy walked in dramatically, stood in front of them and with a slight stutter said, 'Oh! I remember it; I do.' Juni looked at Randy with a mixture of relief and exasperation. He had again got hold of classified information. He said that he would talk to Inspector Singh about it.

The mayor thanked Randy.

Juni said irritatedly that there was nothing to discuss. Cameron gave him a slight nudge and he realized that he was being too mean to Randy and proceeded to say that they might require it later and appreciated his gesture. It was no use mentioning that he too remembered the message. Randy had barged in and spoilt the show.

They talked about the things that had been happening. Juni asked the mayor about tightening the security and he promised some trustworthy gunmen would be positioned at strategic points by the end of the week. Thinking that he had accomplished something and feeling happier, Juni and Cameron said bye to the mayor and Randy, who left for a local fair. Juni and Cameron decided to stay on in the pizzeria for a cup of South Indian filter coffee. They had to try to make sense of all the information that they had gathered.

Their coffee was taking longer than usual and Juni found that he was hungry again. So, he ordered another pizza and a few more doughnuts. Cameron was exasperated and decided to go for a little walk.

Once again, Juni tried to make connections between all the murders. The only connection was that all the victims had been regular visitors of the Prawn Shack. Usually, Juni's mind was energized and happy after a bout of good eating, but this time he was clueless. Juni looked listlessly around. His usually immaculate shirt was creased. His forehead was lined by a frown. Absent-mindedly, he looked around. A young boy of about sixteen came to him nervously, carrying the pizza and doughnuts.

'What's your name, young lad?' asked Juni.

'Jacob,' he said nervously.

'Why are you working here?'

'For extra money.'

'No...I want to know why you are working here?'

'I told you; for extra money.'

'Somebody sick at home?'

'Who are you? How do you know anything about my family?'

'Easy there...don't blow up at me. Your body language gave me the answers that you wouldn't. You blinked rapidly when I asked you why you were here, and you seemed nervous and scared. I want you to tell me your story or I could walk out, no pressure. But I could help you, lad.'

'My mother is very sick. She spent most of our money on my education, so I need money for her treatment... Anyway, why would you care?'

'Hey, Jacob! Have faith. You will get that money. Believe in your abilities and I'll give you a head start. Here is the money for my bill.'

'But this ain't a tip, this is just your expenses....'

'Hold on, don't get too excited...'

Juni looked around. There was one person sitting alone in a corner who he was sure did not know him. He went over to his table and struck a conversation with him. Soon, the man was sitting at Juni's table. Now, he gestured to Jacob to ask for the money from the stranger, then he winked on the pretext of visiting the washroom, and pushed off.

'Always works. Nothing wrong with it! We are all looking for freebies—free drinks, food free—and have to pay heavily for it. Way of the world,' Juni said to himself.

Cameron was right outside the door, when he came hurrying out. She asked him about leads. 'Let's get out of here first,' he said. 'What do you think? That I am gonna go in the pizzeria and come out with the perfect solution? The leads are just a pit leading into a black abyss.'

'Are you okay?'

'Yeah, I'm okay, except for the taste of the mascarpone cheese they used in the pizza. That does get irritating after a while.'

'Okay! What do we do now?' asked Cameron.

'We need to search more abandoned factories which are being used for criminal purposes.'

The next day, they took out the map of the city. First, they would go to the abandoned pharmaceutical factory behind the Guatanimical Bay, as that factory was the most hidden from public view and then the others.

Monroe went to the washroom and puked. He was obviously not well. Juni told him to stay at home.

Juni and Cameron set off on their own. Soon, they reached the factory. Juni pulled out his handgun and entered. The factory was dusty but there were some dust-free areas. He looked at Cameron and then saw two people talking.

'This stuff is great. We got to get more.'

'Chap, I am going for it now.'

'But lie low. We don't want big boss knowing.'

They left hurriedly. Cameron went out back but they

had exited from a rather strange and hidden door. They had disappeared.

Juni and Cameron then inspected the area and went out of the factory. Cameron said, 'Well, this was a bummer.'

'No, it wasn't. Now, we know things,' said Juni.

This was the assembly ground as there was a dust-less patch but almost all other areas were covered with a sheath of dust.

We know where those two people are working.

'Where?' asked Cameron.

'The C.M.P.'

'What? C.M. Pharmaceuticals?'

'Yes, but the C.M. stands for Crystal Meth.' Methamphetamine and amphetamine are used to cure some brain disorders. These are very addictive and restricted drugs and only pharmaceuticals with special licenses can keep them. The C.M.P. is one of them.

'How do you know?'

'I've been there.'

'For crystal meth?'

'No, for cough drops!'

'Forget about it, just tell me how you know that they are working there?'

'I saw their hands. Their nails had a brownish rusty outline, which indicates that they have been getting high on crystal meth.'

'Are you some kind of a chemist?'

'No, I am not a chemist,' mimicked Juni. Together they set off towards the C.M.P.

When they reached the C.M.P., they went in the pharmaceutical store and showed their guns. They saw steps going down towards the basement, the door to which was locked. They broke the door. There were two people there but they were taken by complete surprise and could not put up a fight. They were overpowered and handcuffed. Juni was astonished. Cameron could see it on his face and asked him the reason on their way back. He said that he was amazed at how Cameron had handcuffs ready for use with her. She laughed and said, 'I picked up some handcuffs while you were ogling all the guns and grenades at the police station…more practical, wouldn't you say?'

They went to the police station where they interrogated the first fellow. Juni then took the second one outside alone.

'Jacob! What happened to you?' Juni asked. The second fellow was young Jacob from the pizzeria!

'This guy offered me double the money that was needed for my mother and I thought that it was not a bad idea.'

'Jacob, Jacob, Jacob…'

'I know! I'm sorry, but it was too much pressure and I couldn't handle it. I had to take the offer or else I would not have a mother.'

'Okay, so now listen to me. I will get you home free. Every other day you and I will talk at the pizzeria and you will update me on every development.'

'So, you want me to continue?'

'Yes, you got the money, so this will be the right thing to do. And now hit me.'

'What! Hit you?' exclaimed Jacob.

'Yes, you will take off from here and I will say you hit me and escaped. Now, go!' said Juni.

Jacob pushed off saying that he couldn't hit him. Juni went back into the police station and said that his age was not treating him well and he could not chase Jac...oops! He bit his tongue, and merely said that the guy had run away. Inspector Singh looked at Juni in anger. His nose stud seemed to be glittering more than usual. They had not even got the name of the fellow or taken a photograph. Cameron tried to pacify him. After some time, Inspector Singh was calm and told Juni that such mishaps could happen to anyone but that next time he would not allow Juni to take anyone out to interrogate, separately.

Chapter Thirteen

At their first meeting after recruiting Jacob as a spy, Juni got to know from him that Veron had decided to lie low and not attack during the week. This gave Juni the chance to kick back and loosen the security, though the information was not crucial. After a week, Jacob told him that there would be an attack at the Manheimi mansion.

Juni had not told anyone about Jacob and so, had to come up with a backstory to protect the Manheimi mansion. He told Cameron and Monroe to take the day off. He also told them that he wanted to go alone on a long jaunt. Monroe said that he would go to the market and get some provisions. Cameron looked utterly bored at the prospect and decided to stay at home. So Juni went to scout the area near the Manheimi mansion and saw a man at the top of the neighbouring house. He took out his gun but stopped when he saw the security guard, who had been stationed nearby, 'Take the sniper.' The security guard's .38-calibre bullet pierced the man's gut. He fell down and then, from behind, another man came up with a rifle.

He saw Juni, took his aim and fired. A flock of birds flew from two trees as there were two bullets that had left the barrels of the two guns, and with a thud, a body collapsed to the ground. Juni rushed to the stairs to see if there was any life left in the assassin. Juni's ears were ringing as the bullet had whizzed past his ears leaving a nasty scar on his upper earlobe. He climbed up the staircase making sure that he didn't trip over anything, and as he reached the top, he could tell by the lack of groans and whimpers that the assailants were dead.

Juni went and apologized to the residents for the inconvenience. The owner of the mansion, a much-respected lady, and her daughter had fainted. The local doctor called for an ambulance to take the bodies of the assailants. He asked what Juni was doing there. Juni said, 'Looking for more food joints.' The doctor nodded. '*Typical*,' he thought.

When Juni reached the cottage, he told Cameron and Monroe all that had happened. Monroe was quite impressed with Juni for acting quickly. But nobody in the town knew that Juni had acted on information got from Jacob, and actively prevented a fatal crime from occurring. They all thought that he had been sauntering around looking for new places to eat. His reputation was fast becoming irrevocably tarnished. Not that Juni cared much. He was focused on solving the crime.

The next day Juni met Jacob and he told Juni that the boss

was not pleased at all with the previous day's speed bump.

'Can you ID your boss?' asked Juni.

'No, he doesn't come up to talk,' said Jacob.

'So, where do you meet?'

'Random places—it's different each time. He talks from somewhere else and we hear him through a speaker,' replied Jacob.

'So, I will leave now.'

'But the bill?' Jacob asked.

'Put it on my tab. Nowadays, people know me, I'm pretty famous,' said Juni and sauntered away before Jacob could say anything.

On his way, he came across Randy and immediately tried to weave past him but Randy grabbed him by his arm, throwing Juni off balance.

'It's interesting wha-what happened you know...' said Randy.

'What?' Juni asked, even though he knew precisely what Randy was talking about.

'The Mannheim mansion and the killers and, well, you,' said Randy. He was looking both agitated and excited.

'What about it?' asked Juni.

'Well, I was wondering why you were there,' Randy countered.

'Excuse me?'

'Isn't it strange how you usually don't leave the house to eat alone, and nobody gets these casual holidays, so why now?'

'It was a coincidence, um, a very fortunate one indeed,' said Juni.

'Right,' Randy said. His whole demeanour indicated doubt.

'Okay then, I'll be on my way,' said Juni. He knew that Randy suspected something and he did not want anyone to know about his arrangement with Jacob. He decided he would be more cautious.

The next day, Jacob was in panic. He told Juni that it was his turn to take a shot.

'I have got a message from Veron!'

'Did you get to see him?'

'No, I think he sent one of his men and even he had a mask and a monkey cap. So I could not see him. What do I do now? I should run away. I have no time. I have to take the shot today!'

'What about the gun?' Juni asked.

Jacob said that he had been given a country-made pistol to do the job. After that, he had to dispose of it.

Juni looked at the pistol. It was a rough, cheaply made one. Juni knew that it was not reliable. It might even backfire.

'No, you will take the shot,' said Juni.

Jacob argued.

'You must! I will save the target, though,' said Juni.

'But what if he dies and you are too late?'

'Nothing will happen. Trust me!' said Juni.

Jacob hesitantly agreed.

Juni was there when Jacob got ready for his assignment. But to Juni's consternation, there were guards who had been placed by the mayor to enhance security. One of them saw Jacob and before anything could happen, he was caught. Juni was very angry as he had thought that Jacob would eventually lead him to the killer, but his plan had been foiled. Juni tried to console himself but he knew that this was an expensive mistake. He had sent a message through Monroe to the mayor, asking that the guards be held off that day. So why were they present? Maybe Monroe had not passed the message.

'*What's up with Monroe,*' he thought agitatedly.

Now, Jacob's cover was blown. The guards were kicking him mercilessly. Juni had to intervene and tell the guards that Jacob was his man.

Veron would get to know that Jacob had double-crossed him. Jacob was bruised and very frightened. Juni assured him that he would take care of him. He dropped Jacob at the cottage. Immediately after that, he went to the mayor. He wanted to find out why the guards were there. But the mayor knew nothing. He said that he had not received any message from Monroe. Juni was very angry. He decided that he had to do some damage control immediately. He talked to the mayor about protection for Jacob's mother. And, of course, Jacob had to be placed under his protection. Juni decided that Jacob would have to stay with him till Veron was caught. Thus, Jacob became the newest member of the Dagger 'family'.

It had been a very nerve-wracking day. He reached the

cottage and bellowed for Monroe.

'Monroe! You arsehole, come here!' Monroe came out of the kitchen.

'What happened?'

'Just my mistake that I trusted an idiot to give crucial messages. Did you send the message or not?'

Monroe coloured, 'I forgot! I was so immersed in cooking!'

Juni said, 'The next time, I will make sure you stick to cooking. You better learn some more recipes now that you will be spending more time here. I will not give you important work.'

Monroe apologized but the damage had been done. Juni sighed and said, 'Well, let us taste your cooking...'

Monroe was very distressed and kept saying 'Oui oui.' He rushed into the kitchen to get his dish. But he had forgotten to put on his kitchen mitts. He put his hand on the roast chicken dish and yelped 'OOOuuuii!'

Meanwhile, Cameron had been listening to the whole conversation. She was very angry. 'How can you let him get away so easily?'

Juni was looking thoughtful, 'Would you like to cook all the meals?'

Cameron looked confused and said, 'I don't know how to cook.'

'So, where do you think our delicious *poulet roti* will come from?'

'Well, instead of a French roast chicken why can't you

try an Indian tandoori one?'

'Great, and can you make that?' asked Juni.

Cameron replied, 'No.'

Juni grinned and said, 'Then lady, forever hold your peace!'

He then went on to tell her about Jacob's role in helping him to prevent the attack on the Manheimi mansion.

Cameron was very surprised to hear the story. 'But he looks so young! Isn't he underage to be on the case with us?'

'Yes, he is underage but not too young. He is perfect for the stuff that we need him for.'

'Like?'

'Like climbing up chimneys.'

'Climbing up which chimneys?'

'Yeah, maybe something like that...'

'Forget it! Let's just eat and call it a day.'

Monroe had made some complicated stuff. He apologized again for failing to deliver the important message and to make up for it, he spent the next three hours in the kitchen cooking some really intricate appetizers to the chicken roast.

After eating such delectable food, they were talking happily to each other.

Jacob was not there with them. He had decided to go to his own place.

'Say, Jacob has balls for betraying Veron and coming to us,' remarked Monroe.

Juni looked at Monroe, 'We all develop courage. It is the

situation that gives us courage. And our own necessities…
By the way, speaking of necessities, what is your backstory?
What made you come to this sleepy little port town, which
has obviously seen better days?'

Monroe was quiet for a bit, then sighed and started his
story. 'I was born in Germany and was part of a Jewish family,
but the dictators exploited us like donkeys. We worked for
the neighbour because we didn't want to get caught. But one
day, I discovered that we had been betrayed and the police
were on their way to arrest us and throw us into their camps.
We had lost so many of our loved ones at these camps and
knew the atrocities that went on there. Just as we were about
to run away, the Gestapo came and I hid behind a curtain.
I was very young. My mother had a shotgun. I had already
lost my father. She took aim and killed one officer. Then, she
told me to run out as there was a gap before the rest of the
officers came. I was terrified. How could I leave my mother?
But she shouted at me to obey her last wish. I ran out of the
house. I hid behind a haystack, trying to look around to find
help. I found a huge axe. I picked it up and tried to make
my way back. There were sounds of multiple gunshots. As
I entered my home I saw three officers lying dead and my
mother fatally wounded, lying injured in a pool of blood. The
fourth officer was kicking her. I took my axe and brought it
down on his skull, splitting it into two. My mother looked at
me and said, "Sonny, you obeyed me and protected me. I am
going now. You leave this country and this accursed name, I

command you, and never look back."

'I ran out, and as destiny would have it, found my own kind hiding in the little barn. I joined them. I was still in shock. The group took me in. They had some contacts and we managed to leave the country undercover. I took on a new name, a new language and a new identity. I am Monroe now, the suave French gentleman, an assistant detective. I soon found that there were vacancies in little Indian Meraupatnam, which had earlier been a French colony. I had heard a lot about the town and how it takes in all people as its own... how various cultures and religions cohabit here. I am not originally French, and I felt that living here would be most comfortable. So, I took an opening as assistant detective and reported to Mayor Lebon for my duty.'

Juni was very moved, 'Your story is like an unbelievable tale of dangerous escapades and losses. Who could have believed that you were carrying such burdens from the past?'

Monroe looked at them. Suddenly, he grinned and said, 'You believe me?'

'What? Are you lying?' asked Juni.

'I didn't say that,' said Monroe. The impenetrable veneer was back in place and Juni knew that any further exchange or conversation would only be a banal, superficial one. But he exchanged a bemused look with Cameron and decided to change the topic as Monroe suddenly seemed clammed up. Cameron said, 'Should we have a cup of cardamom tea?' Juni asked her, 'And would you like to make it?'

Cameron replied, 'But I told you, I can't cook!'

Juni said, 'But there is no cooking involved. That's why you make a cup of tea, not cook it. Here, in Meraupatnam, there is scarcely a soul who can't make tea!'

Cameron was getting edgy, 'If it's that simple, I will make it.'

Juni grinned. 'I was just pulling your leg. I will make us a cup and you make, sorry, get the biscuits.'

Suddenly Jacob came running and said, 'Veron wants me…dead!'

Juni came out of the kitchen with the saucer of tea still in his hands and said, 'Hold on! Catch your breath and tell me what happened.' Jacob was panting and looking extremely nervous. He paused, gulped and then said that when he was going to the bathroom to change, he saw the reflection of an armed man with a knife. He had been petrified. He quickly locked the door and jumped out of the window into the alleyway and came straight to Juni.

'"Shirtless or shameless man running in Dormeth Lane" will be the headline of tomorrow's daily,' said Cameron.

Juni laughed.

'Please people, this is not a joke! Someone just placed a huge bounty on my back and you are making jokes!' Jacob cried in dismay.

'Yeah! No, this is serious! That is why I told you to stay here but you had to be brave. Remember kid, misplaced bravery is foolishness,' said Juni.

To which Cameron said, 'Yeah! I bet running around naked on Dormeth Lane was as seriously foolish.'

Monroe couldn't help himself and burst out laughing.

'Okay! So now you are staying with us.'

'Okay! I'll just have to share a room with Cameron...' Jacob joked. For which he got a kick in the guts.

Jacob screamed. Juni said, 'See, I told you, no foolish bravery!'

Jacob grimaced and nodded.

'You are going to sleep on the couch in the living room,' said Juni.

'Fine...'

'And you are our pizza and doughnut delivery boy for life.'

'No deal!' exclaimed Jacob.

'What do you mean? I'll kick your sorry ass out the window,' said Juni.

'Fine,' sighed Jacob.

'Now, go, get some pie.'

'But you said "pizza and doughnut delivery boy".'

'Oh, did I? Make that food delivery boy.'

Jacob rolled his eyes and went away to get some pies.

Dagger suddenly remembered something. He ran out and stopped him.

'Your life is at risk! What? Are you mad?'

'But you said...'

'Never mind what I said and get your butt inside.'

'You are so stupid,' muttered Jacob.

'What did you say?'

'You are a caring cupid!' said Jacob.

'Yeah, that's right.'

They went in the house and Monroe went out to grab some pies.

Cameron started her daily practice (with the little stars) to keep her strength and skills intact.

Monroe got back and they ate the pies (as usual). Then they started asking Jacob questions about the man. He just said that from what he could make out from under the monkey cap, he may have been bearded and not that old. 'Okay, that will help us a lot,' said Monroe sarcastically. 'Anything else?' asked Cameron.

'Nope, that's it. I couldn't get a good look at him.'

'So, let's go to your place to check your bathroom,' Juni said and decided to get moving. He was feeling restless and wanted to work as quickly as possible.

They reached Jacob's apartment. They could not see anything unusual. Dagger paced around the place. 'Tweezers,' he said.

'They are in your pocket,' said Cameron.

'Right.'

He took the tweezers out and picked an aluminium tab from the rug. 'Is this yours?' asked Juni.

'No,' said Jacob.

'So, the assailant definitely didn't think that he would take much time in here and hence underestimated you…'

'Well, thank you,' said Jacob.

'Let me complete what I was saying!' said Juni. 'And so he underestimated your luck. Still, you need to get in better shape. You are going to be facing a lot of these attacks.'

'And how do I get in better shape?' asked Jacob

'Run down to the deli and get me a tuna sandwich.'

'What if I get shot?' asked Jacob.

'Well, your luck is in! Might as well use it to our advantage! Besides, there will not be a second attack so soon… So, relax,' said Juni.

Jacob sighed and ran fast out of fear of getting shot. When he got back to Juni's house, it was locked. He looked around frantically and then hid behind a hedge in Juni's garden and fell asleep. Juni finally got home in the evening and asked Jacob where he had gone. Jacob lost it.

'Y-you guys are bloody crazy! I am a sitting duck for Veron and you take off without me and lock the house?'

'Sorry,' said Juni. 'Oh, and where is my sandwich?'

'I ate the darned sandwich! Now, just leave me alone.' He walked out the house and slammed the door, then came back inside and rejoined them.

'What happened?' asked Cameron.

'I have nowhere to go. That's what happened.'

'What about going to your mother?'

'I don't want to make her a target.'

'No big deal, sit down.'

'I'm hungry,' said Monroe.

'Yeah, let's eat shawarma,' said Juni.

And after about an hour of brainstorming over what they would eat, finally, there was a consensus.

'Yeah, shawarma is fine' Monroe acceded. Jacob said, 'Let's go then.'

'No, you go and get it,' said Juni. Jacob was getting very frustrated so Cameron said that they were just messing with him.

'No, I'm not,' murmured Juni.

Cameron nudged him with her elbow and all of them headed out to eat.

'It seems like our whole case is a big food vacation,' said Cameron.

'Darling, that's how I work,' said Juni.

Jacob ate only one shawarma which led to Juni asking, "Why did you eat just one?"

'Why did you only eat one shawarma? I wish you were this serious during interrogations,' said Cameron.

Juni looked at her dismissively and then looked back at Jacob, who said that he wasn't hungry.

'Pish posh, not hungry cannot be a real thing. Eat one more!' ordered Juni and so Jacob had to order one more.

This time, he ordered from the kids' menu. But Dagger gave him an infuriated look, and so Jacob had to order a full-sized shawarma and stuff himself.

Chapter Fourteen

Meanwhile, Randy was continuing his investigation. Many a time he would try to meet Juni to share information, but Juni was reticent. Years of training had taught him not to pass information on easily. One day, Randy came knocking at Juni's door. He was dressed badly even by his own standards, in crumpled parrot-green trousers and a dirty shirt covered in stains. Cameron looked at him. 'Yes?'

'I have come to give a message to Juni.'

'He is in the bath. Why don't you sit down?'

Cameron looked at him with a mix of distaste and pity and then decided to have a talk with him.

'Why are you always so badly dressed, as if you couldn't care less?'

Randy looked startled. 'That's none of your business.'

Cameron said, 'Mister, it damn well is my business when you are sitting on my sofa and I might have to get it dry-cleaned, so out with it!'

Randy twitched, and then took the plunge. 'Miss, I am not a worldly person. My parents were scientists and I have always lived in my own world. But then there was this girl I loved and I thought that she loved me too...'

'And then?'

Randy sighed. 'And then nothing... One day she came to me and told me that she was getting married. I realized that I had been on a one-way street. I stopped caring then!'

'Do you dress for women? Do you take a bath for women or for that matter, comb your hair, for women?'

Randy said, 'Yes, and so does the rest of mankind. Now that I know that they are not for me, what's the point? Crosswords are easier than women. The hints are proper and if you get the answer, voila, the crossword opens up. But women give you some hints and mean the opposite. No, no, they are not for me!'

'They are like cryptic clues, aren't they? Not a simple crossword.'

Randy exclaimed, 'No, cryptic crosswords have a hidden logic which a sharp, practised mind can discern. But women, ah, they follow no logical pattern.'

'Maybe you have less "womanointelligence" to figure them out,' laughed Cameron and then continued, 'I thought we were talking about your clothes Mr Randy!'

'One and the same thing if you think it through...'

By now, Randy was in the throes of self-consciousness.

He was trying desperately to smoothen his shirt but to no avail and his left hand had found its comfort spot on his ear.

Cameron took out a comb and told him, 'Comb your hair.'

Randy looked flustered. Cameron forcibly put it in his hand and said, 'Go on!' Randy did as told. Now, she told him to turn and look in the mirror. 'Don't you feel better?'

Randy looked brighter. It was as if a layer of drabness had been peeled off. He looked puzzled as he studied his reflection.

Juni came down the stairs and said to Randy, 'More important, do you shit properly in the morning? Because your inner cleanliness is even more important. Tell me, did you take a crap in the morning?'

Cameron thought that Randy would sink through the floor in embarrassment.

Randy surprised her. He beamed and said, 'I take a crap and it is always in proportion to what I have eaten the previous day!'

Cameron almost fell out of her chair.

Juni grinned and winked at her. 'See, I always know how to draw them out. So, what brought you here my friend?'

Randy was beaming. 'You called me friend. I will always remember this… Inspector Singh sent me with a message.' He went on to explain. There had been a crime. Juni had told the inspector to apprise him of all criminal activities in the area. As Randy was near the scene, the inspector had told him to take the message to Juni.

Juni, Cameron and Randy set off for the scene of the

crime. It was the local market and the victim was not from Dormeth Lane. This time, it was a humble townsperson. Dagger looked around. The area had been cordoned off. He suddenly asked for a pen and lifted a piece of clothing off a sharp metal rod which was jutting from a nearby wall. He started asking people if they had seen anything strange. The people who had witnessed the victim collapse said that one minute the man had been heading towards the store and the next minute he had dropped dead.

The inspector, meanwhile, had finished his preliminary examination of the body. He told Juni that the victim, Mr Joseph, had been stabbed on the left side of his spinal column.

Juni looked around and then crouched down before the body.

'He just fell down?' he asked.

'What is that supposed to mean?' asked Cameron.

'It means that he calmly fell down, he didn't scream.'

Cameron was puzzled. 'If a person had been stabbed, then there was no reason for the person not to utter a single sound. What are you getting at?' she asked.

'Whoever killed him used a drug triggered to instantly kill or paralyse his vocal chords,' said Juni.

'Okay, so now?'

'Which means that the killer may work at a pharmacy or a hospital. Otherwise, he wouldn't have access to such drugs.'

Randy said excitedly, 'But the last two arrests were

also related to chemicals—crystal meth! Could there be a connection?'

Juni looked at him, 'How the hell do you get to know all these details?'

Randy grinned, 'Focus and hard work!'

Meanwhile, Monroe had also reached the scene. Juni looked at him and said, 'Just in time. Monroe, get me a list of all the pharmaceutical companies and their workers.' Monroe immediately set to the task.

Within the next two or three hours, Juni was looking at a list of all the companies and their workers.

Now, he started doing some vigorous thinking. 'Okay, so the killer was on a busy street. No one saw him but the traffic would not allow him to go straight down the block after killing the victim. So, he took a left turn. He must have emerged on that street by taking a right turn. All of this, points to the chemist's shop around the block, where the victim was stabbed. Monroe, are there any pharmacies on that road?'

'Yes sir, the Farma pharmacy. They claim that their medicines are organic. But couldn't he have gotten the drug from another shop?'

Randy piped up, 'Yes, but very few chemist shops stock this kind of drug and Farma is one of them.'

Juni said, 'Absolutely right, Randy!'

Monroe was disgruntled. 'If you already knew this, then why did you make me do this useless task?'

Juni replied, 'To find about other chemists that I may have missed. I like to be sure.'

'Let's go and check it out!' said Randy

When they arrived at the shop, Juni went inside alone and talked to the owner.

A short while later, he came back. His shirt was a bit ruffled and his hair was messy. He turned towards Monroe and said, 'Seal this place and call Inspector Singh. Tell them to check behind the brick door in the basement.'

'What happened inside?' asked Cameron.

'I told them that I was with the police and then went down into the basement and let's just say the guy got a bit hyper when I was near the door. But he is not seriously injured. Just knocked out.'

'No, I mean about Veron and the murder! Did you find anything?'

'Oh, yeah, I was right. An employee just quit today. There was some commotion. The guy was shouting. His name was Walsh, Derek Walsh. And he was the store's drug expert. I have his address, which is where we are going right now.' Then, Juni turned towards Monroe and said, 'You go back. You look as if your foot could be hurting you.' Monroe agreed and turned back. Randy shifted covertly and tried to move out of Juni's line of sight so Juni could not spot him and tell him also to buzz off. Juni, however, said to Randy, 'It's okay; you can come, but just this once.' Randy was thrilled.

Randy, Juni and Cameron reached Derek Walsh's house but he was not at home. Only his wife was there. Juni said, 'Derek is not Veron; sorry the mastermind; but he killed someone.'

Mrs Walsh was in shock. She had no idea where Derek was. She seemed to be a sensitive woman, extremely nervous and distraught.

Juni, Randy and Cameron left the house and started walking back. Suddenly, Dagger hit his hand on his head and said to Cameron that Mrs Walsh was having an affair with the victim.

Cameron said, 'How do you know?'

Juni said, 'I can read people's reactions. Didn't you see how distraught she was and how she went into shocked silence after hearing about the murder of Mr Joseph as if she had known him? But she would not admit to us that she knew him.'

Randy pitched in excitedly, 'You are right, Juni. The book series on *Exploring the World* in her house?

Cameron said, 'Yes, what of it?'

'Derek's house had volumes 1, 2, 3, 4, 6, 7, 8, but not 5. I saw Volume 5 in the victim's apartment. I knew the victim, Mr Joseph, and had gone to his house last month. He had a book of crossword puzzles that I wanted.'

Juni said, 'I don't know how, but Derek must have got word of this affair. He kept quiet and then selected a day and stabbed the man at the right time.'

They went back to the house and confronted Mrs Walsh

with the facts. Mrs Walsh was stricken. Her face was ashen.

Juni said, 'Ma'am, I am asking you again. Where is Derek?'

'I don't know,' she replied.

'Ma'am, you don't understand the seriousness of the situation. Your lover is dead and Derek killed him and soon the whole town will know about the affair and murder.'

Her eyes widened in horror. 'He came in just now and asked for some snacks as usual, but I had not gone to the store yet as he was early. He beat me up and went away.'

'Where to?'

'I don't know, he just went away,' said Mrs Walsh.

'Okay ma'am, if you think of something else, please let us know. Derek will be coming back, and so we are positioning a police officer near your apartment.'

'But if he manages to get in, don't panic; just come out to the balcony and throw a cloth or something.' Mrs Walsh agreed.

Cameron, Randy and Juni decided to look around a bit more. But they couldn't find anything more, so they headed home. The police officer waited till late into the night but there was no sign of Derek. It seemed that he had disappeared into thin air.

Randy very sadly said bye to them. 'Can I stay with you?'

Cameron said, 'No, and don't think that we are going to let you come in with unwashed clothes. First, clean up!'

'I'll try. For the sake of this case, I will try.' He put his hand on his unshaven chin and looked at his crumpled trousers and said, 'I guess you are right. I do look like a mess. It seems such a waste of time though...'

Cameron gave him a dirty look. Randy immediately retreated. 'Okay, Okay, I will do the needful.' He went back to his house.

The next morning, the three went to eat waffles and pancakes. They went home feeling uncomfortably full, their tummies all bloated up. They fell right down on their beds. After some time, they thought that they should get back to work. They were not sure if there was any connection between Derek and the spate of killings that had been troubling the neighbourhood. This seemed like a crime of passion. But they decided that they would still investigate it. Randy had decided to go and get himself some fresh drapes, bright blue trousers and a white linen shirt.

Meanwhile, Juni and his pals were busy compiling all the case files. They started trying to see the links. It was a hard and tedious process so they took turns working.

By late afternoon, they had arranged all the files and in the process, skipped lunch.

Soon it was time for dinner. They decided to have sushi. Since prawn had been banned, the Prawn Shack had diversified its menu with tuna sandwiches, sushi and other interesting culinary delights. It was perfect for Juni and company, as they wanted to try something new. While eating, they talked about what to do the next day.

Monroe said that he had to go to the hospital for a

checkup. Juni said that he and Cameron would pay a visit to the mayor.

The mayor was relieved to see them and listened to their updates with keen interest. He was continuously going into 'thought mode' and stopping everyone just so he could think. It seemed very strange. *'Well, he is two bottles down, so he could be making Mozart music out of what I am saying,'* thought Juni.

'Sir, we need some more things for our investigation.'

'Oh! Okay, give me a list. I will place an order.'

'No sir, we need to buy them now.'

'How much cash do you need?'

'The same amount that you spend on about fifty guns.'

The mayor's eyes widened.

'What the…?'

'Yes sir, it is very important.'

'And there is another matter,' said Juni.

'Yes?'

'Well, since prawn has been banned, we have been having a lot of trouble, could you allow the Prawn Shack to serve prawn? We have tried other cuisines but we miss prawn.'

The mayor was looking very abstracted. 'Fine. It was only on impulse that I banned it, since the name seemed to be figuring everywhere. But as there have been no links established, I will give permission.'

Juni was relieved. He could go back to the Prawn Shack and have some good jumbo prawns.

During this conversation, Cameron was waiting outside

and when Juni came out with a briefcase, she was puzzled.

'What is this? Did you rob the mayor?'

'What? No... Are you crazy? I asked for money for the stuff that we have to buy.'

'How much?'

He shrugged and walked away.

'Wait, how much?' demanded Cameron, hurrying after him.

'Just the amount we asked for it,' said Dagger

'What?'

'Just the amount we asked for.'

'What?'

'Just the amount we would need for fifty guns.'

'What, are you crazy? What will we do with all that money?'

'We do need stuff.'

'We need one fifth that amount!'

'Yeah, I know it's just that the other money is for stuff like kobaconkgf.'

'What?'

'Baconrfecre and pizzasfpkn.'

'Oh, my god! Why are you so stupid?!'

'It is much needed. See, I am thinking only in terms of our survival! Now, is that a crime of stupidity?'

'I guess, you are right.'

They walked towards the bacon grill and ordered the most expensive items on the list and a bottle of red wine. As they demolished the array of food and wine, Cameron who was a little tipsy said, 'Look Juni, we should hide all the money!' Juni, mildly irritated, looked at her and gestured to her to keep quiet. Cameron giggled and said that she would heed him just this once.

They started walking back home. Just as they turned the corner of the street they were accosted by three people. They had knives in their hands and they told them not to move an inch or the knives would find their necks.

'Oh, my God! Is that a real knife that you are holding?' said Juni.

'Yes, it is a real knife, now give me that briefcase.'

Juni handed over the case with his hands trembling.

Then suddenly, with a swift kick, he retrieved the briefcase and then proceeded to put pressure on a certain point on the shoulder causing him to collapse immediately. The second one was taken down by Cameron.

The last thug was just staring at what had happened.

Juni took out his gun and pointed it at him. 'O boy, I need to use the gun. I am tired of just kicking and punching.'

Having said that, he hit the thug's wrist in which he held the knife and gave him an admonishing slap.

'Now, tell me, who sent you!' said Juni.

The thug was in pain and crying. He swore that a fellow with a hood had told to nab the briefcase and had promised a good reward. That was all he knew.

'You should not do stuff like this. Now, scoot!' said Juni.

Cameron shouted, 'How could you just let him go?'

Juni made a gesture to her to calm down and said, 'Because I know he is telling the truth and now we will follow him to the stranger.'

They started following him. The thug was running and turned left into the alley. It was an area of dubious reputation, a poor neighbourhood infested with mosquitoes and a breeding ground for crime. He hurried to the end of the alley and entered the house. The click of the lock could be heard.

On the left side of the front door, through which the thug had entered, was a window. It was curtained but he could see through a crack in it. He saw the back of a figure in a black overcoat handing a cup of tea or coffee to the thug. Suddenly, Juni understood. He went back where Cameron waited and gestured to her. With a little hairpin, he picked the lock and both Juni and Cameron stealthily entered the house. As they moved towards the living room, an eerie silence seemed to have descended. They opened the living-room door and saw the thug lying on the floor, dead. His mouth was frothing and there was no sign of anyone else. Juni and Cameron ran through the other rooms and saw a back door through which a cold draught of air was coming in. It was swinging silently as if an invisible hand were swinging it. Juni was annoyed. They had been so close to getting vital information on Veron.

When they got home and saw that Monroe was missing, they started to wonder where he was. Just then they heard something like a knock on their bathroom window. They took out their guns and walked through the hallway. As they kicked open the bathroom door…

…there was Monroe.

'Are you guys out of your bloody minds?' he said. 'Bloody hell, I can't even take a shit in this house without you two spying on me.' He launched into a string of French curses.

Juni and Cameron hadn't stopped laughing and Monroe was already putting on a hell of a comedy show, his scandalized look enough to fuel their laughter. They walked out of the bathroom and settled themselves in the living room.

After a while, Monroe gave up and poured himself a drink.

'That's better,' he smiled and went back to the sofa.

'Say what did you guys eat at your ninja scout camp?' Juni asked Cameron.

'Rice and water and many vegetables.'

Juni took another large gulp from the bottle and sat back down.

'And you Monroe, what did you eat before Meraupatnam?'

'Hmmmmm French food uhm in normal servings… and crepes, loads of crepes…'

'Yo! Cameron,' he said, 'he eats crap,' quipped Juni.

'No, not crap, it's cre…never mind.'

They settled down. Cameron was feeling low. She was sitting idle and gloomy on the sofa. She said to Juni, 'I have a bad feeling about this business. I thought that we were going to catch the killers with a lot of razzle-dazzle but nothing of the sort has happened.'

'So you thought that being a detective is like being in James Bond movies, all action and fireworks and sexy women. Oh! Wait a minute, did you think you were a Bond woman? Wow! Did you think I was James Bond?'

Cameron looked at him and said, 'Maybe…'

'No, no! That's not it. It is drudgery and looking through files and finding a needle among many other needles. It is trying to find connections in a slow, painstaking matter and then, one day, a bullet whizzes past you when you are least prepared. It is like life itself, hitting you hardest with its irrationality when you expect sense and rationality. There's Randy, a total devotee of rationality for whom life is like a crossword puzzle, and then there's you, a total romantic!'

Cameron said, 'And then there's you, the conceited pig!' She laughed. 'But you are quite a philosopher, Juni! I was not prepared for this side of you!'

Juni winked and said, 'There are sides that you have yet to discover, honey.'

'Don't be sleazy now!'

Juni said, 'No, no! That's not it. I was just thinking of life. By the way, where's Jacob?'

Cameron called out to him but there was no answer. Then she saw a hurriedly written letter beside the table lamp. It was from Jacob. It said that he had to leave. He had decided to go far away from the town and let his mother spend whatever time she had with him. Jacob also said that he had borrowed some money from Juni's briefcase, which he would return.

Cameron was indignant, 'The slime bag. He was in the house when we returned and when we were horsing around with Monroe in the bathroom, he stole the money.' But Juni was not disturbed. 'He did the right thing in going back to his ill mother and far away from this town. And as for money, easy come, easy go… I am sure Jacob will return it in his own time.'

Juni was lounging on his sofa. His hair was glowing in the light of the setting sun. The rays shone in through the window and tiny particles of dust were suspended in the air. But he was in his own world, relaxed, quiet.

Cameron sighed. She would never understand Juni at times like this…

Chapter Fifteen

Days were passing. The panic among the townspeople was increasing. Even though the Prawn Shack had started selling prawn, it wore a deserted look as news of the rhyme had leaked out to the public.

One day, Juni said to Cameron, 'Let's have prawn curry for old time's sake.'

'Yeah, why not?' replied Cameron.

They walked up to the Prawn Shack and ordered prawn curry and some prawn crackers. The curry had a typical spicy Indian flavour with lots of curry leaves and grated coconut. As they started eating, Cameron couldn't help but praise the curry. 'I was missing this for so many days. Gawd! I have been dreaming of it.'

Juni was surprised that Cameron was so attuned to spicy flavours. As she was talking to the waiter, she remarked on how such wonderful food hardly had any takers. The waiter looked rather sad and said, 'Ma'am, there was a time when the restaurant was overflowing and our chef was a very busy man, but now we are looking at bad times. Someone has spread an outrageous and contagious and rather distressing rumour, and we are undone. The chef left in disappointment along with his culinary secrets, but we try to manage as best as we can. Even so, we will have to close soon.'

'No, no!' shouted Cameron. The pitch of her voice was out of control. She was delirious. Juni was also feeling very feverish. His eyes were glazed. He shouted and pulled out his gun. 'I will kill anyone who closes this place down. Where are they? The sons of bitches are taking away my prawns! I will destroy them.' Juni was by now standing on the empty table and simulating the sound of gunshots.

Cameron looked at him and then eyed the waiter suspiciously. She knew that something was extremely wrong. The waiter was looking flustered. He excused himself and hurried to the kitchen. Cameron gulped down a glass of water and went after him, and found that she had to try to keep her balance. Just before following the waiter, she had taken the gun from Juni's hand and replaced it with a soup spoon. Juni looked delighted and started uttering war cries and whoops and jumping up and down. There was a crashing sound and Juni found himself on the floor with the tablecloth, prawns and all the cutlery making a cacophony that sounded like an orchestra to Juni's fevered mind. The huge pitcher of water toppled on his head and he was drenched from head to toe.

Juni was clearly not in his senses.

Cameron felt a sense of responsibility to get them out of this sticky situation. She walked unsteadily behind the waiter and hid behind the door. She heard the waiter shout at the cook, 'You dumbass! How much of the ingredient did you put? And why? You should have asked me!'

'But I thought that you told me to put it. You said that we have to ensure that people come back to the shack and we do good business…' the chef was saying.

'Yes! But not so much and not in the investigators' food! You dumb freakin' idiot! We'll have to keep them here now till they cool off.'

Cameron was still a bit unsteady as she returned to the table but because she had not hogged like Juni, she was in a better state. Juni's orchestra, meanwhile, was in full swing. He was hitting the chairs that had suddenly become live enemies and giving a war cry as each one fell.

The waiter came back and Cameron said that she needed to use the ladies' room and seemingly hurried away in that direction. The waiter, meanwhile, put a closed sign on the door of the restaurant. Instead of going to the ladies' room, Cameron quickly turned towards the kitchen door. The cook was standing there, petrified. She stood behind him and put her right arm round his neck in a death clasp. He started spluttering and choking. She said, 'You will answer me and I will give you only one chance and only two seconds. What was in the food?'

The cook sputtered out, 'A drug, ametazamine. It is addictive and I had to put it in each dish.'

Cameron was astonished. 'And why?'

'So that people keep coming back to the shack and we do good business. And then, there were those who got so strongly hooked that we could sell the drug to them at great prices. It seemed to be working till the poem came out. And suddenly, the head chef who was handling all this disappeared, and I was left with the task of administering the drug. I don't have a clue. The waiter usually helps, but today, I did it on my own. I never realized I had given an overdose.'

Cameron twisted his arm and said in a ferocious voice, 'If you want to live, you will run out of this shack and never be seen here again.'

Cameron had broken his arm and he was choking in her death clasp. The minute Cameron said this, he nodded and rushed out in fear. Now, Cameron hurried back to the ladies' room and pretended to come out. The waiter had been trying to control Juni and was oblivious to what had been happening. Cameron gave Juni a lot of water. Then he went to the toilet three times and finally, he was in a better state. Cameron held his arm and they hurried out of the Prawn Shack.

When they reached home, Juni slowly but steadily came to his senses. Cameron quickly updated him on the incident. Juni was shocked, since he couldn't recollect anything. But they had made a breakthrough for sure. The Prawn Shack had been doing brisk business by serving dope to its clients. No wonder, they all came streaming into the shack to assuage their addiction, first unconsciously and later as confirmed addicts. But the mystery remained—why would a string of murders take place? What was the imminent threat? Just for a little prawn?

Suddenly, Juni banged his forehead. The answer seemed to be staring at him right in the face and he couldn't guess it. 'The use of drugs is to paralyse the vocal chords, like Derek Walsh did! It may or may not have been a crime of passion, but what's clear is his proficiency with the drugs. The use of drugs at the Prawn Shack and the factory and all the cartons with weaponry... Can't you see it? The crystal meth...the C.M.P., Farma chemists...these people were obviously into drugs. And that would also explain the murders. Drugs are a big and dangerous business. But the vital connections are still missing.'

Cameron looked puzzled, 'See what?'

'Can't you see that it is all interconnected!"

'But how?'

'That's what we have to figure out... "How?" The key seems to be Derek Walsh!'

'But how do we find him?'

'When in doubt, start at the beginning,' said Juni.

'What do you mean?'

Juni said, 'A shawarma is what we started with, in this town! That's what I mean you dimwit.'

Cameron gave an exasperated sigh and said, 'Okay, you

glutton, I can't argue with you on grub.'

They sat down at the little café and after a lot of discussion, decided to put surveillance on both the Farma chemist shop and Derek's house.

They decided that they would sleep in the mornings and stay up the whole night because Derek would probably be using the cover of the night to move. Cameron asked if Monroe should be given a job too but Juni dismissed it saying that he was not keeping well and that he was also not well trained in martial arts. On the other hand, it might be useful to consider Randy. Monroe was better off cooking his French delicacies. Cameron laughed and said, 'Quite a role reversal!' Juni answered stoically, 'To each according to his or her ability is my motto.'

Cameron said, 'Yeah, so you and I catch criminals and Monroe cooks.'

'And we let Randy in, when we require an extra hand because he is trying really hard.'

'But he always tries hard!'

'I don't mean his work; I mean his dressing!' said Juni.

Cameron laughed. 'What a qualification! He seems to have become your friend!'

'Seems like that,' Juni grinned.

They decided to sleep for some time, so they would be prepared for their night duty.

The first night, Cameron was very excited. She was armed with her shurikens and stars and Juni had a pistol and tranquillizing gun. They took up positions outside the Farma pharmacy and the house, Juni near the former and Cameron at the latter. Randy was on stand by. They stayed up the whole night but nothing happened.

About a week passed. Every night, they would wait and there would be nothing. Cameron started getting more and more disheartened. She told Juni that they were on a false trail. Juni told her that the moment you give up is the moment just before the reward. Randy said, 'But that's a sheer coincidence, that's not a rule!'

Juni said, 'Randy, the minute you understand that life's many coincidences are well wrought in a bizarre logical fashion, that is the minute you will have become a complete detective.'

Randy looked puzzled but decided to crack this crossword of life later.

Chapter Sixteen

After about a fortnight, Cameron and Juni had persisted with their nightly take-outs. Juni now usually accompanied Cameron because she had started dozing off during the midnight vigils. But on this day, Cameron was alone. She had skipped eating as she was not hungry. Juni had said that he would join her after he has eaten his dinner. She saw a faint light near the house. She took a sip of hot coffee from her flask and tried to concentrate. She saw a dark figure open the door of the house and walk inside. The silhouette walked inside. By now, Cameron's heart was beating loudly. She looked around but Juni was nowhere to be seen. 'Damn!' she muttered under her breath. She wondered whether to wait or go inside. She decided that waiting would be better.

After about 15 minutes, the door opened again and the figure came out, holding a bag. Cameron followed him. He walked to the chemist shop. Cameron looked around, but could not see Juni. She wanted to alert him. 'Oh, no! Hope he hasn't eaten some heavy grub and fallen asleep.' As the dark shadow moved towards the chemist shop, Cameron waited. It seemed that he had the key. He opened the door and disappeared inside. Cameron quickly took out her hairpin, opened the door and followed. The shop was in darkness and there was no one around, but Cameron could hear a shuffling noise. She was befuddled. The shop was empty, so where was the figure? She flashed her torch around and saw a trap door near the counter. She carefully lifted it and saw a flight of stairs leading down to a basement. She went down. There was a door at the end of the stairs on the right. She quietly opened it, but there was a creaking sound. Cameron froze. After waiting a few moments, she went in.

She emerged in a dimly lit room with stacks and stacks of cartons labelled, some with labels of weapons and the smaller ones with various drugs, marijuana, weed, opium. It was a mind-boggling array. Suddenly, she heard a voice. 'Welcome, milady!' She tried to turn around but felt the cold nozzle of the gun resting on her nape. 'Now, gently... Don't move milady.' Suddenly, another man appeared and twisted her arms behind her back and tied them. She was tied to a chair. And then the lights were switched on.

Derek came out of the shadows and grinned at her. There was a long scar on his face. It seemed like a villain from a James Bond novel had jumped straight into her life. '*Oh, Bond! I need you,*' she thought, but all she could imagine was Juni snoring.

Derek told the other man, 'Now, be done with the work and then we will see how long this shuriken bitch lasts under our drugs. Paralyse her this time from the neck down so she can't move, but only scream in agony.'

As the man approached her, Derek said, 'No, let's have some fun first. Let's get her high.' They took the opium from the neatly labelled box and injected her. Cameron was feeling giddy and suddenly the world started a technicolour dance around her. Derek then ordered the man to paralyse her. Cameron tried to move, but her hands were tied and she was totally disoriented. Suddenly, there was a sound and Derek looked around. He gestured to the man to go up the stairs to investigate. As soon as he opened the door, a furry thing was hurled across his face. He yelped, as did the furry brown cat. Derek looked angry. He tried to catch the cat which was now running from one end of the room to the other. The man was also trying to catch it. Cameron felt something cold. It was a blade of a knife between her hands. In the shadows behind a carton, she saw Juni. Before she could say anything Juni gestured to her to stay silent. He cut her ropes. Cameron said, 'Bond! My Bond! You have freed me from these bonds!'

The men came charging towards Cameron. Juni jumped forward and took a shot at the man with his gun. Just then, the cat yowled and jumped at Juni and his gun went flying on top of a carton.

Juni had a full stomach and he had been to the washroom

as well, he was completely satisfied. He thought, '*Food—done; defecating—complete...*' He looked around to see the other man still chasing the cat. Derek lunged towards him with his knife, but Juni jumped away. 'Whoa! I'm wearing my favourite shirt, so back off brother!' Juni threw himself towards Derek and tried to jab him but Derek dodged it. 'Quite sprightly, aren't you? Well, I've had a lot of pie so call me lazy, lethargic; let's just talk.'

Derek looked surprised but then he picked up a stool near him and threw it towards Juni, who with a well-aimed punch shattered the stool to pieces and in a flash, and picked up a syringe full of some drug. Before Derek realized what was happening he was slammed face first against the wall and Juni jammed the syringe into Derek's butt.

'Owh!' squealed Derek.

'Do you want want a lollipop or something?'

Then Juni shouted, mimicking Derek, 'Where the hell are you man?'

'Coming!' came the answer.

'Well, I guess, I'll have to get rid of you,' Juni muttered.

He looked at Cameron and asked, 'Do we need the man?'

She said, 'Rainbows here, rainbows there, not a bite to drink...unicorns here, gummy bears there, not a drink to bite.'

'I'll take that as a "No"!' said Juni, and as the man came within sight, he kicked him in the groin and knocked him unconscious.

'You know, about 70 per cent of men die from the

excruciating pain of getting kicked in the balls,' Juni said.

While Cameron was in the land of unicorns, dancing yaks and barking sheep, Juni decided that he wanted some dessert. Cameron giggled and said that she wanted a lollipop candy and pasta ice-cream. Suddenly, Juni said, 'Let's finish this before dessert.' He looked at Derek and said, 'Come on now, out with it before I kick your balls.'

Derek looked scared. He had been given the paralysing injection and so he could not move neck down, though he was absolutely sensitized to pain. He told Juni that he would confess. Juni kicked him and Derek yelled but could not move. Juni grinned, 'Your luck has run out. Now, out with it.'

Derek was crying like a baby. 'Don't strike me. I will tell you all. There is a whole drug mafia which is in operation in this town. The drugs are brought into the port. They are hidden in prawn cartons as frozen food and taken to the Shack. From there, they are taken to the factory and the chemist shops for storage and selling. Drugs and weapons are the two items we deal in and I am the right-hand man of Veron. When the Prawn Shack was used for this purpose, the chef was himself a part of the drug business. Out of sheer evil perversion, he started putting small amounts of drugs into the food given to the customers. They started getting addicted and came back for more. The manager had already facilitated the use of his premises and he was also in cahoots with the chef. He didn't mind getting more business and more money. So, he sold his soul to Veron. Unfortunately, one of Dormeth

Lane's residents overheard the conversation between them, which he told a few other Dormeth Lane residents in a private, closed-door meeting.

Juni interrupted him, 'But how did Veron get to know?'

Derek said, 'Veron knows everything. Thus, began the killing spree. This business is too big and Veron too powerful. Millions are invested. Other countries are supplying drugs and weapons to us. What is Dormeth Lane and a few lives?'

Juni was shell shocked. So, this was the secret. 'But who is Veron?'

Derek said, 'Nobody has seen Veron.'

It was 3 a.m. and Juni was tired. Cameron was tired as hell from laughing. Juni wondered, if he could leave Derek and go to a nearby phone booth to make a call to the inspector. He looked around a little uncertainly. Suddenly, there was a flurry of activity. Randy had reached the spot with Inspector Singh. Juni looked at him in relief. 'Man, do you ever sleep?'

Randy looked at him and simply smiled. Juni let out a whistle. 'Oh, Randy! I owe you one.' He greeted the inspector, whose diamond stud shone in the moonlight. The constables took Derek and his accomplice into custody. By the time, it was all over, the sun was rising and waking up the sleeping town.

Randy took their leave as he had a job to go to. 'I am an accountant and I hate being late,' he said. He was dressed immaculately. Juni looked at him and laughed and said, 'Well, then, now you can go straight to work. No need to get dressed for office.'

Randy left. Juni was now alone with Cameron. He felt so close to the killer and yet so far. They had solved a major part of the mystery but the perpetrator was still missing. Juni looked around and announced, 'That's enough. I am going for a refresher course in problem-solving.'

Cameron said, 'Where?'

'To the pizzeria, where else? We need a fresh mind to think,' said Juni.

As they were walking, Juni looked around. It had been more than a year since this case had begun and it had got under his skin. He looked at the children playing in the park and wondered at the innocent joys of childhood and considered the world—what a despicable place it had become. Unconsciously, Juni detoured and sat down on a bench in the park. Cameron was surprised. But she saw a strange look on Juni's face and decided to keep silent.

Juni's eyebrows were furrowed in concentration and he seemed to be deep in thought. The sweet scent of a lady's perfume was on his mind. Something seemed to be tantalizing him but he could not tease it out. Then, suddenly, the jigsaw started falling in place. The perfume was something that he had smelt on Monroe, but how was that possible? Monroe had been injured and he didn't know Russian, or did he? But he said that he had been in Germany, so where did Russian come from? He knew French and that was it, or was it? Juni was befuddled. It was unthinkable! No, no the poulet that he had made… It couldn't be him! But he mustn't jump to conclusions. One thing was certain: he had to see if Monroe knew Russian. A background check was also required, but how? It would take too much time and that was a luxury he did not have. How Juni wished that he lived in an age when information could be had easily. One flick and the world of information was in front of you. But then, that was all wishful thinking.

Juni started thinking about the case. The mastermind, Veron, had to be lured into a trap. Could it be the mayor. He seemed to be the only one who had access to all information. Perhaps that is all their plans were foiled. But then it was the mayor who had got them to Meraupatnam. And then he thought that the mayor had the letter Y, which he had seen in the signature on the bill at the gun shop. Could Veron be the mayor? He certainly was powerful and rich enough. Juni had his mind set. This was the endgame. He had to set a trap to lure the killer.

One final effort and then he would eat and sleep in peace. He looked at the sylvan surroundings and thanked the powers above for clarifying his mind. With renewed effort, he set out towards the pizzeria with Cameron following him, slightly bemused and puzzled. Pizzas and doughnuts at nine in the morning, when they hadn't slept all night? Her stomach was churning at the very thought but she kept quiet.

'A pepperoni-loaded double cheese pizza and two vanilla doughnuts please!' Juni turned to Cameron and confided in her. 'We are loners and orphans, perhaps that is why the illusion of a family is so endearing to us. Today, jokes and pizzas apart, I am taking you into complete confidence as one family member would another. I hold you very dear to me. I will trust you and I know in my heart that you will not betray me.'

Cameron was startled. She looked at him and said, 'Whoa, hang on! What's the matter with you?'

Juni then proceeded to tell her everything that he suspected. Cameron was flabbergasted. 'I always was a little wary of Monroe. But the mayor, he seems so well meaning!'

Juni said, 'We are now going to lay a trap so that the real Veron can be caught. We have some more work before we can hit the bed. We must spread the word that Derek has some crucial information on Veron and that he is going to give it up. We have to say that Veron is going to be caught by tomorrow morning. Derek is going to be transferred from the town to the state jail at night and there, he will make his confession in front of the higher authorities. He will beg for a mercy plea and has agreed to be a state witness.'

Juni went to the police station. There, he met Inspector Singh, who, after making sure that everyone had seen his tongue ring, told him that Derek would be transferred from the town prison that very night as there was a security threat. This was exactly what Juni wanted. He went into the prison to talk to Derek and while he was doing so, Cameron sidled across to the guard and engaged him in flirty conversation.

Meanwhile, Juni put a drug in his cup of water. As Derek drank from it, he started feeling drowsy.

Juni began shouting excitedly, 'By the king of shawarmas, by the best apple pie, this is absolutely amazing. Derek is going to spill all the beans tomorrow morning.' The police station was abuzz. News spread like wildfire in the town of Meraupatnam. Several news persons rushed to confirm the news with Derek, who was by now under the effect of the drug, and fast asleep. But this time, Juni did not confide in Randy. He was a good friend of the mayor's. Juni wasn't sure if the mayor was involved in any way in the murders. He could no longer trust anyone.

It was almost noon. Juni decided to call it a day. He hadn't slept for the last 36 hours. He told Cameron that they had to sleep now, so that they would be absolutely alert at night. It was going to be one hell of a night. Juni relaxed. He was waiting for some action. Thinking of this, he fell into a sound sleep, setting the alarm, so they'd be up in time for the final showdown at night. Cameron was also still not totally out of the opium influence and was soon sound asleep.

Chapter Seventeen

It was night and the stars were sparkling in the sky. Juni told Monroe that they had extremely important private business to take care off. Monroe looked at them strangely. Juni laughed and said that they had some unfinished business at the pizzeria where they had eaten. 'What?' asked Monroe.

'Oh! I had told them to go easy on the mascarpone cheese that they served me a few days back, but the pizza this morning was fantastic. And I want to congratulate the waiter.'

Monroe said, 'Of course, I understand how important that must be!'

Juni grinned and said, 'I also want another slice of the pizza. Cameron, hope you are ready to share with me!'

Cameron said, 'I am famished! Let's go. Would you like to come, Monroe?' He declined and said that he would rather stay at home.

Just as they were about to leave, Juni asked Monroe if he

could make poulet the next morning for breakfast. Monroe said, he was not sure. Juni and Cameron exchanged an uneasy look. Juni held Cameron's hand and squeezed it gently.

Juni and Cameron set out. Cameron was looking glum. Juni looked at her with raised eyebrows. 'Is this the last night before we solve the case and have to part?' asked Cameron.

Juni looked at her, 'Only if you want it that way...'

'What do you want?'

'Do you have to ask?'

Juni took out his gun and double checked it. Cameron was ready with her shurikens and they set off towards the police station in the motor car they had hired. They were sure that there would be an attack on Derek that night.

The station was quiet. The telephone wires of both the mayor and Juni's house had been tapped. Cameron had connected them to the wire near the police station. She set her equipment near the telephone pole. They both waited. Cameron was listening carefully to each sound. Suddenly, there was a shuffling and the wires came abuzz. Juni listened carefully. It was the mayor talking to someone. He seemed to be giving curt orders. 'You will finish Derek off before tomorrow morning. Yes, and remember there is no room for failure.'

Cameron's eyes widened in horror. The mayor, the most respected man in this town, was Veron? It was unbelievable! No wonder, they had been reaching dead ends all the time. They had been running to him with all the information they had been gathering. And who could his helper be? It couldn't be Monroe, as they had wired Juni's house too and there had been no suspicious call yet. Cameron heaved a sigh of relief. Still, they decided to remain near the telephone line and keep a close watch for anything suspicious at the police station.

A police van with iron bars on the windows crept into the night. Juni signalled to Cameron to be ready. They waited with bated breath. Juni edged closer to the van under cover of darkness. Everything was calm, eerily so. The guard came out of the van and walked towards the police station. Soon, Juni saw him coming out with a handcuffed Derek, who was extremely groggy as the effects of the drug had not worn off yet. There didn't seem to be anything untoward happening. Everything seemed very much under control. Juni looked ready for any attack on the vehicle. Cameron was making sure that she had the back of the van covered.

Juni approached the guard. 'All okay?' he asked.

The guard nodded and opened the door to let Derek in. The door closed. The driver started the car. Juni stepped back. Something did not seem right. He was feeling extremely uneasy. He ran a hand through his hair and looked around once again. On the surface, there seemed to be no obvious threat. The van started and Juni looked at Cameron. She was gesticulating wildly. He quietly and stealthily moved towards her. She whispered fiercely, 'Can't you smell it? The sweet smell of the ladies' perfume?' Juni was stunned; so that was what had been vaguely nagging him! Cameron had caught it. He turned and saw that the van had started moving. He ran towards it. Cameron took two stones, expertly rubbed them together and placed a twig that she had snatched from a nearby bush. The twig caught fire and with her metal star, she hurled the burning twig towards the van. The van jerked and stopped. Using this distraction to his advantage, Juni leapt on top of the van.

As the van started again, Cameron threw an iron blade to him. Juni caught it. It would have sliced his hand in two had he missed it. Muttering some oaths under his breath, he carefully bent down after planting his feet firmly on the roof. He was now spread-eagled. He bent down, and started cutting away the iron bars of the window. With the razor-sharp blade, this was done very quickly and silently. The van stopped in a desolate spot. It was miles from anywhere. There was a gunshot. Juni almost jumped out of his skin only to see the guard's body being thrown out of the van. The van started again.

Juni could hear Derek groaning and moaning and sounding pretty much incoherent. Juni took out the iron bars and slid into the van. He gestured to Derek to stay quiet, but Derek was beyond understanding. The van came to a screeching halt. Carrying a loaded pistol, the driver opened the door of the van. He saw Juni. He looked at the other vacant seat. There was nobody there. Juni had pushed Derek out the window a mile or so back.

Juni looked at the driver. He could smell the perfume. He

leapt at him but the driver took a shot and the bullet went through Juni's arm. Juni flung the iron bar at him and the gun flew out of his hand. The driver shouted something in Russian and came charging towards Juni, but Juni was calm. He took out his gun and fired. The driver moved aside with the reflexes of a panther. Juni was amazed at his quickness. He was losing a lot of blood and had to do something fast. The killer came towards him with deadly intent. He was brandishing a blade in his hand. He swung it towards Juni who ducked and picked up a handful of mud and flung it at his face. 'Eat that, you filthy wretch!'

The killer screamed. His eyes were stinging, and suddenly, out of nowhere, there came a metal star which was flung with deadly accuracy. It fixed him to a tree. Juni turned and saw Cameron. She had run at full speed down the road till she reached Derek and then almost dragged him along.

'Oh, boy! I am glad to see you!'

Cameron grinned, 'I picked up Derek on the way.' She took out her chains and ropes and tied the driver up. Then Cameron tied a piece of cloth to Juni's hand to stop the bleeding.

Juni said, 'It's only a superficial wound, nothing to worry about.' He grimaced as he spoke.

Cameron said, 'But hurts like hell, I can see!'

They turned their attention to the driver. They peered at his face, and saw to their chagrin that he had on a thin rubber mask. Cameron said that it had to be carefully peeled off to reveal his true identity. They slowly removed the mask, and the whole time the killer was grunting and shaking his head. But when the mask came off, they were totally shocked. They were still not ready to believe what they were seeing. Their suspicion was confirmed—it was Monroe!

'What a betrayal!' Cameron gasped. 'You were French, sent to help us. You were our friend, Monroe…'

Monroe spat out the remaining mud and said, 'There is no friend in this world… Let me tell you the remainder of my story. When I found friends, they sold me to the Russians and from there to here was a long path of crime. The only true relationship is one with money and power.'

'And look where that led you my friend, behind bars. You were better off cooking French food and pretending to be friends—better and happier. What did this game of crime and power give you? But I am sure that you will have a lot of time in jail to think about it,' said Juni sadly.

'But we are all playing, aren't we?' asked Monroe.

'Enough of this bullshit. You go to the prison. Yes, that's where you will go,' said Cameron.

Juni looked at Cameron. She was looking very fierce. Her brown eyes were glinting in the dark and her movements were short and precise. They held a lot of anger kept tightly under the leash of her ninja discipline. She looked at Juni's wound. The cloth had become soaked with blood. Cameron said that it was better than it looked. The bullet had not lodged itself in too deeply.

Juni asked Cameron, 'If Veron was talking to Monroe, how come we didn't hear Monroe on the microphone? After all, our phone was also wired.'

Cameron said, 'Maybe that was why Monroe kept going out on mysterious errands: to talk to Veron. Sorry, the mayor.'

'Well, we have to be totally sure. He has to be caught in the act with irrefutable evidence and witnesses.'

'So what do you suggest?' asked Cameron.

'Have you got something to eat?'

Cameron looked at him incredulously. 'What's wrong with you?'

'Nothing, just hungry,' said Juni, straight-faced.

Cameron sighed and dug out a salami sandwich from her bag.

'That's a good girl; now, we have reached a perfect understanding,' grinned Juni as he wolfed down the slightly soggy and out-of-shape sandwich. Then he gulped some water and said, 'Okay, now I am ready.' Monroe was watching all this. Juni took his rubber mask and put it on him and said, 'Now, time for some drama!'

They sat back in the police car with Monroe tied up and went straight to the police station. Inspector Singh was pacing about very agitatedly as there was no police officer on duty. He couldn't leave the Police station and didn't know exactly what was going on. It was time to tell him everything. Inspector Singh was shocked that the mayor might be Veron. Moistening his lips and giving his tongue a wiggle, he said,

'He is such a respected man. Why would he jeopardize such a respected and luxurious life?' But even though Inspector Singh was dazed, he cooperated. Juni had put on the mask and then he went to the mayor's house. Cameron took her position near the telephone wires. The inspector got the electricity cut off in the area near the mayor's house. Juni now put on the rubber mask and knocked softly on the door. The door opened.

Juni said 'The job is done. Derek is dead.' The mayor pulled him inside and whispered fiercely, 'Why did you come here? How did you know?'

The mayor said, 'Good, you will get your payment shortly.'

Juni was the perfect voice impersonator, and the dim light made him pretty much unrecognizable. He said, 'But you have everything; why would you do this?'

The mayor's face transformed. He gave a diabolical smile. He had a gun in his hand. 'You are gonna die. You thought that I would let you stay alive, the only person who knows Veron.'

Juni was amazed at the evil being who stood before him. He mimicked, 'How can you kill me? I did all that you asked and more!'

The mayor laughed and said, 'Because now, I will find another to take your place. Because I want to go on murdering. I am the lord of death and crime. The invisible lord, but now you have seen me. I tried to keep my identity from you, but you guessed. Well, this is the first and last time you will see me. Feast your eyes!'

Then, the mayor said, 'But how did you know that it was me?'

Juni replied nonchalantly, 'Just some educated guesswork. You wouldn't talk to me at Juni's house and I had to go out on some pretext each time that I had to talk with you. You knew everything happening there even before I told you. And finally, your voice tantalized me for days till I could finally recognize it.'

The mayor started laughing and his face acquired a grotesque and frightful look. 'Okay, Mr Smarty Pants, I'll show you who I am. I love money. I love feeling powerful and though I have everything, it can never be enough. I need my daily fix and I need to feel in control. I can control the lives of people as mayor but I control death as Veron, and death is an exciting matter.'

His face had an eerie glow and Juni knew that Veron was not in it for money. It was the attraction to death that pulled him, and how he could control the lives of others. Juni felt fear for the first time in years at the sight of such unadulterated evil.

Veron pointed the gun at Juni's temple and said, 'The brains or the heart? You have the choice.' Juni grinned and said, 'The balls, that's where it will hurt the most.'

Juni had been in sticky situations before but this was by far the stickiest. He had a split second and if he was late then well, it was bye bye to life. All these thoughts were flashing in his mind. He tried to divert Veron. He used his own voice.

'Hang on, I am Juni, Juni Dagger! How can you not know, who you are killing! I am doing you a favour by not letting you kill me in ignorance.' He removed his rubber mask. The mayor blinked but his hand was steady on the gun. He knew that something had gone terribly wrong. He grinned diabolically. 'So you think that my game is up? You will not be alive to see me win Juni, tough luck.'

He started to pull the trigger, but Juni had no more surprises up his sleeve. He felt a moment of fear. Suddenly an ear-piercing sound came and there was a loud thud. Veron turned in the direction of the noise and fired. There was another ear-piercing scream of agony but Juni only needed a fraction of a second. He lunged at the mayor and there was a furious scuffle. It was semi-dark and the scream now sounded nearer. It was Randy, his arm bleeding, and he was screaming loudly. Veron had injured him but his vocal chords seemed to be on a roll.

Juni had snatched the gun out of Veron's hands. Meanwhile, Inspector Singh came inside and Cameron, sensing that Juni was in danger, had left her post and rushed towards the mayor's house. The inspector pointed a gun at the mayor and said, 'Hands up!' sliding his tongue out one last time before all this was over he continued, 'Mister!' The mayor took one look at him and knew that the game was up. Cameron threw a metal star at him and pinned him to the wall.

Juni looked at her and smiled.

Veron looked at him. The shock was apparent on his face.

He said, 'Yes I made an error in calling you to investigate. I thought that I would enjoy the game. But it went too far. Next time…'

Juni guffawed. 'Mister, there won't be a next time!'

The electricity had been restored and Juni had raided the larder and was chomping at some chips.

Randy was in shock. His beloved friend was the killer. Juni said to Randy, 'You are so clever, but you made two errors. One, never think that life is as rational as a crossword puzzle, and two, never think that your friends are above suspicion.'

Inspector Singh studied Randy's wound. He called for an ambulance but not before commending Randy on his work and promising him a part-time job as an investigator. Randy was thrilled. He had been shot in the left arm so he could not lift it to his ear, though he had a desperate urge to rub it. 'Hey, Juni, could you just rub my ear please?' he asked.

'But why are you not using your right hand?' asked Juni.

'No, it doesn't feel the same. Please rub my ear with your left hand,' replied Randy.

Juni grinned and was about to oblige when a furry creature jumped into Randy's lap and started licking his left ear.

'Why, hello there, Buddy! Good to see you again!' The brown shaggy dog of indeterminate breed was wagging its tail. Randy looked at him delightedly. 'Juni, meet my new friend and housemate, Buddy. Buddy, this is Juni, my mentor. This is Cameron, who taught me how to wear good clothes.'

Cameron laughed and said, 'How do you do? Nice to meet you.'

Buddy was in true form and offered his paw!

Then turning towards Randy, Cameron said, 'You are a good student and the next time we see you, you will have a girlfriend.'

Randy was blushing. The inspector said, 'The ambulance has come. Randy, you need to go now. Buddy can accompany you.' Then he turned towards the mayor. 'And it is prison time for you.'

The mayor was taken away. The inspector shook hands with Juni and Cameron and said that he would commend them for their bravery and diligence in solving the case. 'You have done an everlasting service for the people of Meraupatnam. You are our guests. Please feel free to stay here for as long as you like.'

Juni and Cameron were now alone in the house. The police force was doing its duty and cordoning off the area. Juni turned towards Cameron and asked, 'Do you have something to eat? I'm famished. Even a soggy salami sandwich will do.'

There was commotion outside the house. People had assembled and were cheering Juni. He seemed to have become a hero. Mr Crow could not take the adulation. He whispered to his companion, 'Much ado. He took so long to solve the mystery, and ate too many pizzas and doughnuts and left unpaid bills.'

Lilly was also standing nearby, and looked at him. 'You

are a mean and petty person, Mr Crow, to be saying such a thing. Mr Buchner is far braver and more generous. He risked his life for us and all you can do is be jealous and petty.'

She saw Mr Buchner looking at them with sad eyes. She waved merrily at him and called him. 'Harry, my dear, come here. Let's go on a date. Shall we?'

Mr Buchner was flushed with happiness. He held out his elbow, which Lilly took hold of. They started walking. Mr Crow looked at them and saw Lilly was quite out of his reach now.

Juni was sitting on the sofa of the mayor's house. He had found a nice yoghurt dip to go with the chips. He offered some to Cameron. 'What now?' asked Cameron.

'What? Maybe pizzas and doughnuts?'

'No, I didn't mean that...'

'Then, what?'

'Don't be dense...'

'Dense?'

Cameron got up, 'Okay, good luck. I better get going.'

Juni looked at her and said, 'Right, where will you go? Want to come with me to Delhi?'

Cameron looked amazed, 'Delhi?'

Juni grinned, 'Yes, for my next assignment. I have heard the food there is worth trying.'

After a moment of utter silence, Cameron turned and looked around, and before she replied Juni said, 'Stay.'

They sat on the bench and talked about how the bag of

chips could be improved by a cool ranch flavour.

'You have crumbs on your lips, let me get that for you,' said Juni as he drew her close. Their lips brushed against each other, and the rising sun made it look like a scene straight out of a cheesy romantic movie.

Acknowledgements

This being my first foray into book writing, I am indebted to: first and foremost my mother, Jyoti A. Kathpalia, who encouraged and inspired me to write and has been my first critic; my sister, Anya Kathpalia, for her insightful comments and observations; my father, Arvind Kathpalia, for his support and encouragement; Sunita Gupta, Principal of Air Force Bal Bharti School, Lodhi Road, for her faith in my ability to drive this project; and Ayan Pande for the feedback.

I take this opportunity to express my heartfelt gratitude to all my friends in whose company I found wit, whacky humour and interesting insights into life.

For making this book possible, I want to thank: my publisher, Kapish Mehra; Dibakar Ghosh, Editorial Director of Rupa Publications; my editor, Ananya Sharma, for her unflinching support and invaluable inputs; and Gauri Kelkar for her indispensable suggestions.

Last but not the least, I thank you for picking up this book and hope you liked it!